Revolver

BY COMMON CONSENT PRESS is a non-profit publisher dedicated to producing affordable, high-quality books that help define and shape the Latter-day Saint experience. BCC Press publishes books that address all aspects of Mormon life. Our mission includes finding manuscripts that will contribute to the lives of thoughtful Latter-day Saints, mentoring authors and nurturing projects to completion, and distributing important books to the Mormon audience at the lowest possible cost.

Revolver

Stories by Heidi Naylor

BCC PRESS

Some of the stories in this collection were originally published, with small differences, in the following:

New Letters: "Revolver."
The Idaho Review: "Language of Desire."
The Chariton Review: "A Season of Curing."
Sunstone: "The Mandelbrot Set," "Name," and "Jane's Journey."
Dialogue: A Journal of Mormon Thought: "The Home Teacher."
Detours: A Writers' Anthology (The Cabin, 2013): "Mack and Natalie Have Gotten Very Comfortable in Idaho."
Moth & Rust (Signature Books, 2017): "Lucin Trestle."

The story "Jane's Journey" includes several lines from "The Lady of Shallot" by Alfred, Lord Tennyson.

For information contact
By Common Consent Press
4062 S. Evelyn Dr.
Salt Lake City, UT 84124-2250

Cover image: Monica Galentino (*https://unsplash.com/photos/zjk0Tx6-M6Q*)
Cover design: D Christian Harrison
Book design: Andrew Heiss

www.bccpress.org

ISBN-13: 978-1-948218-00-9
ISBN-10: 1-948218-00-3

10 9 8 7 6 5 4 3 2 1

To Patrick,
whose strength and kindness persists,
alongside his advice:
"Did you remember to put in
the gratuitous sex and violence?"

Contents

Acknowledgments   ix

Revolver   1

Language of Desire   12

A Season of Curing   26

The Mandelbrot Set   48

The Home Teacher   71

Mack and Natalie Have Gotten Very Comfortable in Idaho   102

The Hardness of Steel   110

Name   133

Jane's Journey   147

Lucin Trestle   172

Acknowledgments

I'M SO GRATEFUL to BCC Press and to the magazines and editors who first published these stories. Many thanks to Boise State University's Department of English and MFA cohort and program, specifically Brady Udall, Mitch Wieland, Alan Heathcock, Elise Blackwell, Kerri Webster, Anthony Doerr, Bruce Ballenger, Robert Olmstead, and the late Al Greenberg. Thank you also to Karl Beus, Daniel Woodrell, Stephen Carter, and Lisa Torcasso Downing; to the Virginia Center for the Creative Arts, the Kimmel Harding Nelson Center for the Arts, Starry Night Retreat, the Idaho Commission on the Arts, and the Alexa Rose Foundation.

For writerly friendship and expertise, workshopping, encouragement, and support, I am grateful to Joan Boren, Susan Bruns Rowe, Jana Herbert, and the late and beloved Kelly Holmes; also to Amanda Bennett, Mollie Ficek, Elizabeth Lester-Barnes, and Christi Nogle of the Sawtooth Association of Women Writers. Above all, I'm thankful to my family for boundless love and constant stories.

Revolver

MEMORIAL DAY, Klink's daughter drives him to a gathering at the state of Idaho veterans cemetery. The day is bright but chilly, with a motion- and cloud-filled sky and a long row of flags at half-mast, whipping and snapping in the wind. His cane doesn't bother him much, only on lawns and near skateboarders or smiling women. He refuses the offer of a golf cart. Finally, carefully, they take their seats.

Some rows ahead of them, the senator's words blow back from the dais and over the graveyard. No matter, he's not much of a senator, has put the state through a round of grief and embarrassment. People look away. A small phalanx of horses is sat by men in the varied uniforms of armed service branches. The horses' tails are tidy, braided and tucked, their bridles glossy, no blinders, and especially at such distance, they seem not even to blink. Horses and men—wait, he thinks, one of the mounts is a young woman—all straight and still as sculpture. Klink's gaze lingers a moment. The breeze revives, thick enough to make his eyes water, but its wash of cold fresh. So many of his pleasures have become small, fugitive and beckoning. Little sensory favors.

He lets his vision travel. Stringbean biker couples with matching braids stand in leather chaps, fringe fluttering, hands in one another's pockets. The fragrance of their cigarettes, so often unwelcome, seems somehow appropriate here. Big-headed tulips huddle and bend, their faces not yet open. Children run and jump from boulders. A voice rises: *Lan*don! Get back here *now!* Down the hill, a ponytailed man in pressed denim stands, eyes to the restless sky, hands clasped behind his back. He guards a headstone where a woman kneels in silence.

America. America.

Which welcomed Klink (it was more than he'd hoped for): a German ex-patriot, who fought long ago on the Russian front in what he called "the only war." Unteroffizier Heinrich D. Klinkenberger. Future husband, future father of an American daughter. Now a widower. A courteous vet of forgotten loyalties, in a nubbly cardigan, with the cane and a dachshund and sometimes a quiet companion for dinner. No grandchildren, which he supposed was a mercy.

In that war those long years ago, he had one afternoon surprised a woman in a roofed-over cellar near Otradnoye. He is startled to find that after all these years he can still see her. His mind unfolds a vision of her face, the wide pale forehead. Her mouth. She was thin, and blond. The tulips . . . everyone foraged for tulips; their odor of moldy onions filled her damp cellar. She had composed a gray soup with the bulbs, using water from a well and adding bits of hay, no doubt gleaned some pink, vaporous dawn when the field near the train station might have looked merely fallowed, not burned over, ravaged. The cellar walls were lined with newspaper.

His commander gestured, a little chop with his hand and a single grunted syllable, not to be mistaken: that Klink should kill her. At this, her eyes flicked to her right, toward a shadowy corner, then lit on Klink and settled into a steady gaze. She did not cry or beg, but lifted her chin and held out the bowl of soup. The commander laughed. He shook his head, and she placed the bowl on the floor. She reached into her blouse, then, around toward her back, and the commander took her hard by the shoulders and shouted in her face. *Nyet,* she protested, and then whispered, *nyet,* and he allowed her to bring out a piece of folded lace. She shook it before them: a shawl, a scarf. The new fall of dust made her cough.

Klink knelt quickly and took a revolver from inside his boot, where it had been strapped in a hard shank against his shin. He tried for the thoughts that he understood would strengthen him. She was stupid. Buying them with an embarrassing souvenir. She was conniving. Perhaps his job would be easy. A kind of poetry, using this gun instead of the government-issue Kars he'd been carrying. He stood and palmed the cool handle of the revolver. A thin band of muscle on her neck appeared and throbbed. She lifted her hands, first to Klink and then to the commander. He knocked the lace from her hands, and it fell into the bowl.

A small noise, then. The light was poor, but Klink's attention turned again to the corner. Two children there, shadows, unflinching. Genderless, colorless. Their eyes made him think of bum lambs on the farm, the ones with no mothers. These children seemed to be phantoms, little more than exhalations of dusty air.

So much black dust, ash, soot: it had been everywhere, and some days the sun couldn't cut through it. Klink settled, half a world later, in this small western city with clean rock gardens and bright skies. His name shrunk to Henry. And later, to Hal. Hal Klink. He'd thought a truncation was necessary, but it wasn't. Americans, God love them, they'd forgive anything, and in not much time. He married Marjorie, a woman with plump hands and a creamy, fluttering alto in her laugh, a woman whose round chatter could chase off any sullen brooding. His daughter's class had included a Heidi and an Anneliese; as he tended his lawn, he saw that his neighbors owned a VW and a Kawasaki. No one, it seemed, cared about what he had done in the war, which side had been his. Sides, loyalties had blurred with each passing year.

Over time he'd been able to shorten his memories, too. But as this Memorial Day wore on, discomfort gathered, as it will in an old man: the familiar hard knob at first, in the small of his back; then a shifting, roiling burden in his shoulders that grew and boldened and settled, soured in his gut like a body in a field, and he felt it had been lurking, festering, waiting for a day such as this. At home that afternoon, he staked peonies and swept his patio, called his little dog and fed her bits of canned sausage from his fingers. These efforts tired his body but not his mind, and before long he found himself driving back to his daughter's.

She is newly divorced, this daughter, and he's taken to spending occasional evenings at her house. Early crickets sing outside the window of her den. Tonight he is too depleted for any more patriotic themes; they watch a program she's recorded, about lacemaking. Tatting, it's called. The kind of program she liked, after a long day at the hospital. Another time, it might have bored him. On this night the program seems to him to be courageous and insistent in its simplicity, audacious and direct. Assuming, as it does, that anyone will take interest in a gentle task with no end but beauty.

His daughter is not beautiful, and had not been. But the way she cares for him, her small attentions—the morning gathering, the cup of tea at his elbow, seasoned with alcohol and set on a bit of pretty cloth, the golden light in her den—these seem to him touching and worth noting, if such an art as lacemaking is worth noting. Klink feels that his daughter's flat face, her thick body, cased in coarse skin and dotted with moles, has been too heavy a sorrow to her. These flaws have made him impatient with her at times, unfairly, he knows; tonight he can acknowledge that they are also a comfort to him. He wants to tell her what he's not thought of for years: forget beauty. Find it somewhere else. Look at the broad, changing sky, hear the rustling leaves in the night, touch the cool silver of the teakettle. Adjust the lace at the window. Look no further, please God; don't look beyond these. He wants her to understand that beauty gets a woman traded, possessed, passed around for a pack of cigarettes, for a dented can of peaches. For nothing.

In the cellar, the Russian woman had been beautiful. And, of course, possibly treacherous. She opened her blouse and lifted out her breast: pale and delicately veined—almost translucent—he'd actually thought of the slowly inflating barrage balloons on the Dnepr, and recalled now the lovely curve of her and of them as they began to rise, nearly glowing, associated with dawn and naked light and no longer distinguished to him as enemy, whether Russian woman or Russian weapon. At her action, the commander laughed, a short bark, and motioned: *Ach, Klink, ja! See how she demands you. Take your time.*

He heard the unspoken imperative: *finally, you'll be a man. We can stop carrying you.*

Heard also the commander's relinquishment of first rights to the woman.

This was clear in the way he dropped his cigarette and ground it with his boot, saying he would wait outside the cellar. *Die Kriegsbeute*, he said, wearily, as he climbed the stairs. The spoils of war. More dust sifted through slats of weak sunlight as he let the wooden door fall shut.

Klink couldn't look any longer at the woman, though he felt her eyes on him. Time slowed. He lifted his fingers, clammy with sweat, off the revolver one by one to cool them in the stillness. He wanted to dry them on his leg. He wanted to wipe them with the lace.

She closed her blouse and hugged herself. He and she might still be there, face to immoveable face, covered in ash, if she hadn't spoken next.

"Give me the revolver." Her German was intelligible. Her bearing regal. It could have been that she was disgusted with him. One of her hands found the strength to reach out, and as he recalls this, the shimmering call of crickets outside the window of his daughter's den seems to halt. Absently, he stirs the air with his trigger finger.

His thoughts are ghosts, cold and whispering, directed toward the wall in the low golden light, into a print of Don Quixote on the ragged horse. Klink was an old man who'd been, really, just a smooth-chinned farm boy called up to fight, for the Fatherland, as the Americans told it, though he notes this with no apology; only with the assertion of essential heart and terror and, too, the core of certainty revealed by his action, by what happened next. He thinks of grown men his daughter has described, big men with ropy forearms and tattoos, whose lips revert to suckling as they lay unconscious on trauma tables.

In the cellar, he'd handed the woman his Nagant, the Tsarist weapon he'd been so proud to carry. Taken it from a soldier in Smolensk, in a scene to be recalled another, braver day. For many weeks, it had been strapped to his shin, where it had worn a scab on the ridge of his bone. Never even fired it, been saving it. He gave it over to her and almost dared to hope that, in the growing mishaps and unexplainable chaos of each day, it had come now to be poorly loaded. Even mistakenly unloaded. As though were he unready, the war might stop.

But the woman. Who also—despite her composure—needed to stop the war. She acquired an expression of deepening calm as the revolver emptied its load. The thin bodies of her children, their blurred breaths suddenly audible, catching, lengthening, halting. First one shot, then the next; then, without breaking rhythm, a shot fired into her own heart. He reached to break her fall and his face filled with the hot taste of gunpowder, the metallic smell of blood.

He straightened her legs on the cellar floor and took the revolver from her fingers and began to recall that one of them must still try to breathe, and he was that one. He laid the children next to her, one on each side. As he stood, he cursed himself for hoping, on his own behalf rather than hers, that his commander wouldn't come back down the stairs.

His limbs are pressed, weighted into the armchair. Every cell of him exhausted, scoured by the memory, one he hadn't seen through in years. Long time ago his fingers made a shroud of Russian lace; now, tonight, they are stiff and cold, worrying the knotted leather buttons on his cardigan. Worlds ago. A story never told, a story all but lost to him.

His little dog whines. Next to his armchair, the thin curtain at his daughter's window swells in the night's breeze, and there's a rising flourish of wind in the street. It carries another sound, one he has also not forgotten.

He parts the curtain to reveal a horse, a great muscled beauty, stamping and snuffling, stepping high, its rider in silhouette against a cone of streetlight. Klink clears his eyes, blinking; he can see no details, but becomes aware—the trick of memory, again; can nothing be lost to him?—the rider wears the uniform and cloak of a cavalry officer. Beyond the horse, across the street, stands a motionless corps of infantry where earlier a house had been. The horse pivots, begins to trot, to canter smoothly past a stop sign. The breeze lessens, and the hollow *t-tlot, t-tlot* of the horse's hooves grows more pronounced. Klink, alarmed, afraid the horse will stumble on the slick surface of the street, wants to cry out. He worries he has done so.

And perhaps he has, for now the officer pulls up and whips the horse around. Back they come, toward his window but still on the street. The horse slows to an elegant high prance and tosses its head. A buckle, a ring on the bridle jangles softly. Together, the horse and rider move in lengths of shadow, behind a picket fence, before the body of men. So beautiful as to be ethereal, and Klink can see the moon coming forward, through clouds and darkness, flashing on the rider's sword and again on the glimmer of the asphalt, as though the street were paved with stones. The officer reins in his horse. Halts, and turns to regard the face at the window. For a moment all is still, and then the officer lifts his fingers to his cap. The horse nickers, and Klink moistens his lips with his tongue, ready to speak, but there are no words, no words for the silver, the brightness of the rider's cloak, its billow and fall as he holds his salute.

"Dad?" An intrusion, alarmingly on cue. He's forgotten where he is. "Dad?" she asks again. The words are soft and insistent. The warmth of the room, its furnishings, his daughter, all the hard edges of where he is click piece by piece into focus.

"Freshen your drink?"

Klink shuts his eyes briefly and tips his head. It's grown late. He lets the gauzy curtain fall. He gets to his feet and begins to collect himself. His daughter's voice speaks concern, what might have annoyed him and made him want to kick away his cane.

Not tonight. Tonight as he raises his eyes, hers catch the light. He cannot look away. They capture him; they remind him that you never can tell but what a woman has a little beauty stored away someplace for safekeeping. Leaning on the cane, he touches his thumb to his daughter's cheek, where—yes—there's a little bloom yet, and his thumb stops its tremor. He puts his hand gently to the tender cords at the top of her spine, and for a moment—truly—he is strong and young, and home, and she is so lovely, his lissome little girl; and all around the world, commanders stand at ease, that some measure of charm be retained in the hamlets and valleys. He leans in to kiss her forehead.

"Well now," she says, and sets herself to brushing his shoulder, straightening his collar. Her mother's low, sweet flutter in her laugh. "We're quite the pair."

Language of Desire

ON THE AFTERNOON school bus, and without thinking about it, Larkin Brousseau ran a finger over the bump and down the crooked bony ridge. She wondered if her nose had been broken when she was little—perhaps at the playground, or the neighbors' trampoline—and no one at home had noticed. Or if they had noticed, they'd figured, Hello, it's a nose. It isn't sliding off your face, or wrecking your mobility: it will heal by itself. People in her family rarely went to see the doctor. Why would you want to hear a doctor say, Sure enough you've got a broken toe/sore throat/bad cold/ case of flu—that'll be ninety-eight dollars.

Plus there was the sense of what God willed. God rarely required doctors, who were there to help you into this world, and sometimes to help you out of it. Handling the in-between was pretty much up to you. Not that the in-between didn't count. Oh, it mattered—insofar as your personal priorities. Your obligation to faith and obedience. Larkin couldn't really bring up the fact of the nose. Such a concession to vanity would highlight a character deficiency, a distortion of things that mattered.

And there were so many people worse off. Every day from the back of the bus drifted the odor of joints and cigarettes and sometimes burning hair and always something metallic, rain-soaked. Blood. That was what she imagined it to be. It made her nauseous, but she left the back-of-the-bus crowd alone and they returned the favor. They weren't the worst, anyway.

Worst was picking up Mickey Overby out on Rushton Road. Mickey was short and quiet. He didn't seem to bother anyone; but no one on the bus ever let him sit down. A few times he had tried, got the edge of his hip onto a corner of vinyl, his feet splayed on the gritty rubber tread of the aisle as though to say, I'm not really in the seat. But someone—Teague Jolovich, a total jock, or Marcus Holski, a brainiac who used to go to Catholic school—someone like that would walk up to the seat where Mickey was perched and say nothing, just stare at the *No Smoking* sign at the front of the bus like it meant something. Flick his eyes from the sign to the clear plastic cup in the holder, where the bus driver periodically dropped her cigarette butts.

And every time, Mickey would stand up, and Teague or Marcus or whoever it was would take that seat. No grin, no glance exchanged, just that straight-ahead stare. Mickey's hair was soft and filmy in the back, bed-headed, stuck in clumps like a frowsy bottle brush. People called him "Sludge" as in *Let's go, Sludge, haul ass.* High school was a horrible place full of horrible people who did horrible things to one another.

Also her skin was going schizoid. Breaking out in angry, wet-looking red cysts that throbbed. One on her cheek that burned if she lay a finger on her jaw. Two on the other cheek. One placed exactly between her eyebrows, like she'd glued it on for decoration. And a smattering of others, in varying states of eruption and decay.

Earlier that day Larkin had joined six girls in the auditorium, skipping class and sharing fingerfuls of peanut butter straight up, from the jar, as they talked about big sex with the wrestling team. Michael, Dorian, Willis, Eddie, Falco, and Jarvis, sweaty, tight-skinned boys always hawking bubble-spiked loogies at the vents in the grass-trimmed, concrete foundation of the gymnasium. The girls jockeyed for revelation of the most telling details. The taste of mustard and Tootsie Pops when Eddie kissed. The licorice veins on Dorian's forearms and biceps. The sweet talk of Jarvis—"You, baby, you *always* the top of my list." Listening, Larkin found she was touched with envy, but she also couldn't quite believe what she heard. Then Lorri Sandmire said, Hey girls, did you know? She nearly punctured her plump lips with her teeth as she said it. *Fucking* clears the skin. She tipped the peanut butter jar toward Larkin. Honey, you're not getting any.

At dinner, Larkin said to her sister Katrea—truly, she thought, with intent to be helpful—you have food on your face. Katrea looked up and said, Well, you have zits on yours.

Yet in the upshot, nightly before the mirror upstairs, Larkin could actually ignore all this. And if what she did was not exactly to ignore, then it was that she could talk herself out of the problem. Okay, I have six zits, the LAST six, the FINAL six, I bid you no welcome for the duration of your existence, and when you go, you are the END. Tell your friends to stay away. Bring no more.

God. Please.

Don't let me get any more zits.

See. I'd be pretty. Look at my golden brown eyes. My to-*there* lashes and caramel-colored hair. My *distinctive* nose. I am the color of a Keebler Honey Graham.

Please, God, let me have beautiful, graham-cracker-colored skin, I'll do good in this world every day.

She puckered her lips. The auditorium six were experts on beauty as well as sex. According to them, a girl could attain a dangerous pout by leading with the chin and saying, *Wogan.* Bizarre, I know! said the prettiest one, Audra. She had leaned in toward Larkin, her breath like sweet apples, and whispered confidentially. Not smarmy or superior. *But models swear by it.*

Wogan. Larkin said it to the mirror. Wogan, yes? She dispensed with the pout, lifted her arms like a dancer, and stepped toward the open window. Its filmy curtains fluttered, and she drew the word out, a call into the churning night. *W-o-o-o-g-a-a-a-a-n-n-n-n.*

Her voice on the breeze, but a cruel nothing from the velvet darkness. Instead, the triple-shaded, thrift-store lamp at her hip winked. It had a weakness in the wiring. Like her, the lamp was flawed but serviceable. Here Larkin indulged a fantasy, a fair one, and not without restraint: that wiring would jigger loose for good in three years' time and burble up an orange flame that would catch a burlap window dressing in her own sophomore-year college sixplex. Surprising to note that the fabric will simply melt at first, curling upward until—*pffft*—gone, in the same way cotton candy disappears on a warm tongue. Then the building will hot rot from within and begin an accelerative collapse, flushing out the unscarred and undulating form of that same Lorri Sandmire, who will be living on the third floor and have made the unlucky choice of skipping her afternoon classes to grease the sheets with a married hubcap salesman named Brucey Wentworth, champion bowler of eleven perfect games at Ackley's. They'll escape, naked, screaming, to take cover in the rain-spattered blue plastic tarp of a passing-by geologist, who unearths it from the sample-strewn bed of his pickup and apologizes for the shards of gypsum and calcite crystal that cling to the thready nubbled patches of white where blue has worn away, jabbing Lorri in all the wrong places. No one else at home.

Another wink. And Larkin breathed deep. She felt extravagant, expansive, bold enough to call again into the night, and again she went unanswered.

But though she could not have known it, the winking light in Larkin's window found a target. It was picked up by seventeen-year-old Silas McInerney, who'd set up an impromptu camp in the forty-acre tree- and boulder-studded field to the north of Larkin's house.

Silas was a young man of sober persuasion who answered the lamp's anonymous, faraway wink with an arbitrary sequence of dots and dashes from his telescopic Mag flashlight. He drew the beams long on the dashes, made the dots especially sharp to account for what felt like a viscosity in the air. He shifted his knee, which had been grinding a rock into the yielding ground. *Aaaah*, better. A lone cricket chirped a plea, it seemed to Silas, for the peace of summer to linger, and he counted the number of chirps in a quarter minute, added forty to get the temperature. A trick he knew. He liked to guess the temperature, liked to figure the number of hours until sunrise. Eight and three-quarters. He appreciated knowing there were around twenty billion years to go until the earth cooled and imploded. A lot of time; not forever. Soil, grass, water, sky, all were touched, then, with some small measure of urgency, despite the warm blanket of darkness, heavy, complete except for Larkin's lamp. Silas wondered idly—and, he thought, perhaps stupidly—about the distance between his light and the lamp, though he did not know it was a lamp. Did this distance have much effect on the light's travel time? That answer, and so many more, he would have to look into.

He wanted to fuse his fascination with the obscure and the trivial with something more consequential, or at least more practical. To be part of arguments and issues of the world. This was best expressed by his desire to go to sea, perhaps to join the Navy, and learn to park a submarine, a slender tube of gunmetal steel and whirring props, in the deepest of the cloudy depths. There, he suspected thought could become distilled, the mind laid bare, stripped, *essenced* to its most durable minimums. He thought of surfacing, the whooshy animal sound of the sub breaking topside among icebergs in the North Sea, or perhaps near the tip of India, where on the docks awaits a raucous boil of color and noise. His mouth watered as he pictured a yellow plate of curried potatoes, topped with petal shavings of curled cucumber and a dollop of oil-swirled yogurt. Served up by a lithe, careless, swivel-hipped waitress with black eyes and skin the color of caramel.

Though high school had been lackluster (some spoke of him as a possible late bloomer, a kid who could go either way), the notion that he might be unsuccessful in the Navy, or whatever sharp-shot path he'd claim, never occurred to Silas. The wiry density of his limbs, the force and pull of his shoulders, the speed and pickup of his legs, his light and useful mind: he could have sensed the bright energy in these features individually and never understood them; but when he considered himself in the aggregate (it was rarely conscious), he believed he was not mediocre. He had possibilities, despite so much outside evidence to the contrary: his smallish frame, his looks (certainly of no consequence), the persistent ignorance of girls and, more to the point, he felt, of teachers and counselors, who never once met with him to go over test scores or college apps.

He likewise did not have average desires. No. Since he can remember, his head has been filled instead with thoughts of slick, hard edges. The chrome-lined fins of classic cars, the cutting runners of bobsleds, even the beveled angles of unframed mirrors; and newly, lately, the compensating clefts and swellings of the outdoors— pockets and hills of loam, brooklets and streams, even the saucer-sized lacy faces of wild carrot in this untamed pasture, lit faintly by the moon. Camping was a new and surprising pleasure. Dot-dot-dash. Flash.

And the wind picked up an undertow of coming rain and sent a shushing breeze, tinged with bouquets of bunchgrass and poplar and catching him full on the face. Soft air. A fragrant, feminine wash of air, as warm and wel-coming as the word *air*. The lamp's light winked again, and Silas checked the tattered booklet of code he kept in his jeans pocket. What message could he send, to capture this night? What smoking candle? *Propel*. No. *Cruise*. Surely not. Finally, and laboriously, Silas constructed his message. *Hurry*, it said. *Hurry*.

Nothing from the distant lamp. Eventually, its light disappeared. Another mystery. And Silas's surprise at the quick surge of gladness that gripped him across his shoulders and down his arms. This was what he had come for. With this the empty fields had beckoned. He clicked off the Mag light and lifted his chin to the cloud-filled sky. Eyes closed, mouth open, he let the satin breeze wash over him.

At this moment it did not occur to Silas to match his yearnings with anything, anyone female—the waitress, the bedroom lamp notwithstanding. To whom did such a connection occur? To his mother, Charmaine, who was awakened by the same gusty wind, perhaps the flash of lightning. Or the partnering low growl of thunder, which underscored the chime of silver pipettes hanging from gossamer threads on the gazebo beyond her patio. Charmaine, in a pink seersucker bathrobe, had been dozing in her bungalow on the other edge of town, about twenty miles south of Silas, soaking her feet in warm Palmolive and resting her head on a leather . . . a fragrant leather . . . oh, *shit*, it was her leather-covered Bible, catawampus on the thick round arm of her loveseat. Now its onionskin pages were crumpled and creased, the spine loose, nearly ruptured, and, what was almost worse, she'd lost her place. Some backlit and holy passage in Numbers: sweet savours, ephahs and hins of beaten oil, bullocks, continual bread, censers, flesh-hooks, badgers' skins—the stuff of opulent dreams, into which she'll never quite tumble the same way again. Her idea had been to use these lonesome evenings when Silas was on the prowl (this was where she made the feminine connection) to finally slog through the two testaments once and for all. Seized by a lasting impulse. After all, she'd long called herself a believer.

Could the litanous punishments and excesses of those books have explained the motivating force of Charmaine's early life? It was fear. When Silas was born, she touched her lips to the rosy, velvet skin just past his forehead, where his baby pulse faintly throbbed. Up, down, up, down. Such a whisper-thin membrane. She murmured low, *You'll never play football, and you'll never go to war.* Wrong on the first count, touch and go on the second.

She married from fear of not being chosen. And that earnestness rightly killed her marriage. So she tells herself—lighten up! things are not so dour! But the reality is different. The reality is that her husband's cruelty—often budding, but explainable in light of global warming, traffic, indigestion, crabgrass, and ATM fees—finally, fully, flowered, with a cutting Monday night comment about deadbeat dads being a clear sight more honest than your goddamn suffering madonnas who made such a pageant of their bad choices. Charmaine looked at their baby, kicking away on a blanket spread over worn carpet. There'd been some ruckus earlier, and no shortage of mess and smell and noise and trouble. But just now his mouth popped open and shut in little oohs, and he worked them up into a cry of . . . well, there was no other word for it, it was a cry of *joy*, at the yellow circle of light on the ceiling, at the deep, shadowy corners, and at the sweet rapture of wanting to kick your leg, hard, like *that*, and *that*, yes, you *are* kicking it, nothing like it, this round-limbed, well-oiled body. What a relief, for Charmaine, to have found her line. By Thursday, she and Silas had moved to her mother's. Eventually she could afford this small house.

Into which one man or another would, at long intervals, come for a time and then go. Yet not before his healing wonder at some untended feature. Her slender waist (average, at best). The crisp and oily brown edge of her German pancakes ("It's in other counties, ma'am, they call that burnt"). The roundness of her kneecaps ("fits exactly in my palm") and the arch of each bare foot ("too pretty for words"—okay, she'll give him that). She missed the particular heft and grapple of a drilling contractor from Baltimore who plied her with bad poetry, which she laughed at—and, because it was offered so frankly, came to appreciate. But not as much as she did his denim jacket, flannel-lined and never washed so the fabric felt like moleskin and buttery leather and carried the particular odor that was him: menthol cigarettes, beef jerky, the skin of a baseball, and, most especially, motor oil.

His name was Tom Tucker, which in itself could make her smile, and he finally did go for good: a job, a contract in deep Montana, where she did not follow. To be honest, she was not asked, and did not offer. In unguarded moments, Charmaine could admit that he'd have been a good father to Silas. Over the course of several weeks, when Silas was about twelve, Tom had taught the boy to pitch. Charmaine watched from the kitchen window, through the slatted sides of the gazebo. Silas, sullen and unwilling at first, until he finally brought the ball down, and one merciful day she heard Tom say, Hey. *Hey*. That was okay. That was not bad. Charmaine could recall the sunlight, the brisk and easy voices. The comfort. She'd looked down at her hands in the soapy water. It was a thing with men, she knew, women with dishwater hands. A caretaking thing, a domestic power dynamic. Dishwater blonde. Soap bubbles as jewelry, or maybe as chains. She shook off the thought.

Still, such a pleasure, and not easily won: when she broke a pitcher, or ran out of that dish soap, she could go buy more with money she'd earned herself. Her professional work was uninspiring; she kept books and prepared documents and proposals for a small commercial and clean-room architecture firm. But her salary had improved steadily, and she'd just had the house repainted. No debt. A well-maintained car in the driveway. Silas with new sneakers and a room with posters and a sound system and a clean, though secondhand, desk. She was sewing a flannel

23

blanket for him to take camping, to line his sleeping bag with. Working on it an hour in the lamplight each evening.

These years later, it could still come as a surprise to Charmaine that she had, after all, made for them a life. Was there room in that life for Tom Tucker? The day of the pitching there was. Certainly some nights, God help her, there was. But no room, no time, no capacity in her for it to go bad. Fear was a preservative, after all. It had its blessings, along with its cost. It had its own sweet savour. The thought carried a touch of the obscene about it. What did Charmaine care? She slid her damp and softened feet into a pair of fuzzy pink slippers. She padded over to the closet. There in the back, obscured by the ironing board and Silas's outgrown baseball uniform, hung Tom Tucker's denim jacket.

Which she slipped on. She wrapped her arms around herself. The denim cuffs dangled down beyond her hands; it was like being hugged by an invisible man. Charmaine closed her eyes, thinking of the blind man's game she had played with Silas when he was little. She inched her way through the maze of cozy living room furniture, to the French doors that opened onto the patio. *Sweet savour*, she whispered— and the sibilant sounds were borne away on the breeze, into the night and its slipstream, its trailing, filmy strands and strains of connection. Sweet savour, again—

And, really, this was what she might say to Larkin Brousseau if she could. If anyone could relieve the strange and pitiable, the unintelligible . . . yearnings . . . regrets . . . doubts that were to be found in the daylight way Larkin walked, the way she could drop her eyes and watch the ground, the way she tipped her shoulders forward. For how was somebody like unfortunate Mickey Overby, like Larkin, like any number of people, like she herself, Charmaine and how she had seemed—how was a body to know she would survive?

Charmaine could guess. Charmaine, a witness, who'd seen how things that happen won't be halted, *she* could suppose. Silas, or someone equally untrammeled, unfettered, would let his assurance touch its match to Larkin's (who'd just now watched his Morse sequence with a mild curiosity). He would give and take her love, he could coax her out of herself.

But even this—utterly human, and thus unreliable, as Charmaine well knew—even this was not necessary or requisite. All that seemed essential was the occasional cooling and unsettled night: the quivering hush of the fields, the trimmed grasses, the patchwork yards with their careful bark dust, their lucky garden gnomes and delicate chimes, the streetlamps and the silver sky. The varied and transitory calls into darkness. The lit and haunted language of mercy.

A Season of Curing

SUCCESS parts its curtain and makes way for the specialist: the daughter of refugee parents (Persian, the noble, northern Tajik tribe) in small-town Virginia, who determines at eleven that she'll be a physician, at sixteen that she will focus on developmental disorders, and by her thirties has established a renowned medical center for research and treatment of Williams Syndrome. The Idaho farm boy who, as he hauls sprinkler pipe over mounded rows of sugar beets, spins eloquent, hand-shaped arguments for and against farm subsidy legislation, setting in motion achievements that will secure him a seat on a federal bench before he has his first gray hair. The organist who wakes day after day at two a.m., discomfiting neighbors and occasional guests, to practice in complete darkness and just out of the clumsy surrealism of her dreams, the better to sharpen dependence on her ear and its relationship to her touch.

The outdoorsman who drops out of a Michigan university and hitchhikes to Maine to revive the crafting of birch-bark canoes—after the manner of the Penobscot Nation, who have unthinkably allowed the technique to languish—each canoe requiring a thousand hours of handwork. People do things. It's the lament of the people who don't.

And the partial, unspoken regret of Ripley McCord, on the eve of his fifty-eighth birthday. It seems to him that over the past few weeks he's been inundated with examples of human efficiency, determination, passion. He is more than twice the age of John Keats when he died. Easily past two-thirds of the time he can expect to live. Oh, blast, he thinks, and wonders if it's anything close to what Keats might have said. Probably not.

Why did he agree to meet for drinks? He and his ex-wife, Margo Knopfler McCord Hennis, are seated on high stools at the Midshipman. Chestnut Hill, just outside Philadelphia. Margo's a professor of Romantic literature at Temple, and a devotee of Keats, which is why Ripley is haunted tonight by the figure of the young, driven, consumptive—canonized—poet. Margo's eyes shine in the gold lights of the bar. She's describing the newest crop of graduate students in her cadre. Her crepe-y, suntanned fingers are wrapped around her glass.

"What's gone wrong with them, to make them so mild?" she says. "Where is their passion? I miss . . . misbehavior.

Those riotous times that got us all in trouble. We've all become a little too tight."

She adjusts her shoulder seams, loosens the bow adorning her blouse. After a few more drinks the bow will be hanging in two wrinkled, dejected banners from her shoulders and the blouse will be partly unbuttoned— there's a stir in Ripley's crotch at this thought—to reveal a gold serpentine chain that dives down the stretchy skin between her breasts, toward her subtly thickened waist. A sight to deepen his sadness. He needs to make a gracious exit before that happens.

" . . . so mannered," Margo continues, "so coherent and polite, so conscious of their charm. They're on time for everything, wouldn't dream of making anyone wait. They raise their hands in class." She looks at him. "I have a theory, you know."

Ripley manages a smile. Margo's theories.

There was one she had termed the Margo Embargo. She'd told him, when their marriage hiccupped over the last two or three graceless years, ending with his refusal to share an inheritance, that he was a cliché—"stuck in grade school, hoarding a locker-full of candy bars and carnival tickets," stopping by to have a look "for his own reassurance." He'd parked the money, a modest fifty thousand, in a solely owned money-market account whose balance he checked weekly. If she'd done the same, he was sure, there'd have been no problem.

He's partway through a plate of bratwurst and cabbage, scooping mustard and broth with a crusty roll of rye, wishing for another glass of ale. He's been successful, by many standards: towing business, commercial real estate, Toyota dealership. He knows how to make money, is tight-fisted and smart but also restless. Each business was sold to fund the next.

The last venture was a salvage company he formed to procure the lumber from a submerged railroad trestle out West, in Great Salt Lake. And he had made money: the trestle wood was strong and beautifully cured, sold mostly to artisan cabinetmakers and craftsmen—more specialists whose work he admired. Now he's trying his hand at financials. Investments, CDs, loan-to-values. Styleless work, bland and stodgy coming after the trestle wood. Still. Financials will hold him until something else catches his eye.

The waitress touches his arm and pours more ale. He thanks her and listens absently to Margo, who prefers to speak in whole paragraphs. Is it too late for him to focus? To specialize in anything?

Peripherally he notes the presence of others in conversation at the counter and at tables scattered around the bar. A young man is standing by the door talking to another man when a blonde, heavy-set woman makes her way to the exit, shrugging her cardigan over her shoulders. Her purse bangs against her hip. The man, still in conversation, steps back and pushes the door open for her, his fingers splayed wide on the gleaming hardwood. He nods at the woman, who thanks him and steps outside.

The gesture is small but impeccably gallant. Ripley's eyes linger, watching the man see her through, watching the way the woman's hair catches the streetlight. Perhaps he knows now why he has come. After a woman expresses her displeasure with the way she's been treated by a man, he wants to compensate with something nice. It's not simply to assuage his guilt. No. It's that such overtures make a difference for people. Pubs, parties, gatherings. What better places for wordless apologies than these? He signals the bartender with two fingers, nodding toward Margo.

For her, for tonight, he won't indulge his flirtation with despair any further. Even Margo knows it is his turn to say something.

"Now hold on a minute, before you shrink these defenseless and—" a raise of his eyebrows here—"*absent* young adults." It is not, after all, so difficult to respond.

"Seems to me they've already embraced a bit of fire," he continues. "Don't forget, you're tending a hot-blooded group intent on the Romantic poets. 'Old, mad, blind, despised, and dying kings' and 'electric poisons, flames out of her looks into my vitals coming.'" He jabs his fork into the air. "Have I got the general gist?"

"Good, Ripley, very good." Margo plucks a peanut out of a pewter dish. "I'm glad the whole of me was not wasted on you."

"No," Ripley says, with a sigh. "Never wasted, sweet." He smiles. "I know you too well. Your classroom is a yeasty hotbed for the seeds of rebellion."

What? he thinks. Too much, too sexual. Much too much. Why, with Margo, does he persist in saying the wrong thing? Now, look, there she is, tipping her head back, laughing at him. She wipes tears from the corners of her eyes. Will it be possible to back out gently, change the subject?

"Your students are in the right place. Fortunately society places all the blame—and credit—on parents. Not teachers."

They'd decided not to have children. Parenting—all the risks and adjustments—it was too lengthy and arduous. Had sidestepping a family been a good decision? He stifles a sigh. Tonight he's as moody and changeable as the adolescent they'd so consciously avoided. Their past seems remote, suddenly, his next comment safely distanced from it.

"How is it, though, that you seem to have spoiled me for other women? Somehow chained my restless heart to your . . . "

Margo wrinkles her nose. "What? Picket fence? Oh, *don't*," she says, turning away to sigh into the smoky air.

She draws her shoulders up and breathes out long and slow with her eyes closed. It's a motion of hers that he'd forgotten, so self-protective it makes his chest ache.

Ripley is astonished to find that he is not simply speaking with affection. In fact he feels tender toward her, the wife of his reckless youth, the early choice of his heart. There's a gate they both know better than to reopen, the path back to her explosive rages, her nudgy, week-long silences. To his spare, tender words—he knows how to speak to a woman—but they could never quite mask (for her) a distant regard. A frozen courtesy. Possibly he had been overly selfish, like she'd said. "You're always so preoccupied, arriving, taking your leave, so incredulously remote, concerned with your own satisfaction. I might as well go out and feed the pigeons all day for all you ask about it"—and petty, too, about money, clutter, cooking.

He'd felt he could be a good husband if Margo would simply play along, if she'd be happy enough to share his space with him.

It turned out her goal was not that he be a good husband. Her goal was—imagine!—more to do with her own life and the way it touched and melded with his. It could even have been that her goal was to be a good wife.

Nevertheless. He supposes he and Margo are destined to grow old in a faraway sort of together, phoning one another out of the blue, as she had done this afternoon on the eve of his birthday. "Have you got plans tonight, Ripley?

Because I would like to buy you a drink. You know. Another year . . . past the pier"—this for him, not a lover of poetry, instead speckled with a groaning, perverse appreciation for the contrived rhyme, useful for measured breathing in preparation, in hope, for sleep: "In secret we met / In silence I grieve / That thy heart could forget / Thy spirit deceive." Margo could no doubt name the meter for him.

And no, he certainly had no definite plans. Sweet of her to call. It turns out he likes her, so long as his dose of her is infrequent. She smooths her skirt, picks at a piece of lint on her knee. There are a few new freckles on her hands, the bones stand out more sharply than before.

It comes to him at this moment—from the thought of that tender inheritance and what it had cost his mother to provide? From Margo, who has unmistakably aged?—no matter, he knows what he can specialize in. Generosity. That's it. The milk of human kindness. Munificence. Bounty.

He knocks his knuckles on the table.

The broody feeling is lifting, its vague unease spirited away not by the brass and glass of this pub, not by the ale, not even by Margo and her darting conversation.By his new specialty.

"Do you think you might be romanticizing youth? The feeling of having time, being indestructible?"

She considers. He's always appreciated this about her: the careful, measured response. The way she takes her time.

"They don't have any idea what they've been given, do they?" she says, narrowing her eyes.

He snorts. "Of course not," he says. "None of us do." Maybe she's been having the same feelings he has, about specialization, lost opportunities. Perhaps such ideas are simply biological, like attraction, though what physical purpose they serve he can't imagine.

He takes a drink. "They'll squander their youth and beauty."

A grimace flickers across her features, which compose themselves into something like determination. She looks pretty, in a contradictory way, her pensive, damp eyes and dusky lashes. The generous impulse surges up through his torso, a dark, blood-filled flush.

"What surprises me—and no laughing at this, please— is the lack of appeal young women have for me."

She does laugh, too loudly, her face tipped again toward the ceiling. "Right," she says.

"No, really," he says. "Okay, they can be beautiful. But—"

"But what?" she asks, on the edge of anger. "But you have to eventually get out of bed, right? And have a con- versation?" She sets her glass down with some force and shakes her head.

It's partly true. The older he gets, the less patient he is with young women, their pouts and demands, their moods and their messiness.

"Lord, I'm so tired of it all," she says, speaking to a spot past his shoulder, and very softly. "Of trying to figure out how to do this dance with any of you. What was it my mother used to tell me—'why buy the cow when they can get the milk for free?' I thought she was so simplistic, but now I think she was dead-on. Ripley, isn't it time to grow up?"

He has to press down his annoyance. How was it she could still so ably misconstrue whatever he said? He'd wanted her to feel desirable, and not old, though he didn't want her to think he was coming on to her himself. He meant only well. A gentleman. Thinking of her.

This generosity was not going to be easy. Intention was clearly not enough. Possibly it could cause a good deal of sorrow. Probably it could never be faked.

Margo excuses herself, "to powder my nose," and as she walks away, she sees a couple she knows at the bar. He watches her nodding, chatting. Her quick recovery, her wide grin. It comes to him briefly to wonder if she's planned this, orchestrated being seen with him. He drops his eyes, tucks into his plate like a high-schooler, not wanting things to get complicated, not wanting her to point him out. As far as he can tell, she doesn't. Good. Good.

But then, oh Lord. Shame steals across his shoulders, the chagrin of assuming he holds an elevated importance in her life. How scornful she would be if she knew. He wonders now if she'd been aware of the women he'd turned to during the unhappiness that was their marriage—two women, each he had loved for a time. Recalling this is not sweet, and it has moved beyond regrettable: the women themselves had seemed like kindnesses, too, on his part, when they happened. Happy, hapless, happened. He is not a cad. He is not.

Yet glimmers of memory crowd in—honey-colored hair, the swing of a bold red coat—"a bit of flamenco, a jolt to the senses! but, Ripley, do you think it's too much?" (*Yes*. And what woman in the world wanted an honest answer to her question?)

The other woman, quite beautiful, her black hair swept into a chignon. She had cooked for him simple and graceful meals and never ate them; not eating was the central compulsion of her life. If you didn't eat, you were not only clavicly outlined and stylish; you were impossible. It was like the Shakers. If you didn't consummate—the elegant term was in this woman's honor, he knows she'd have been pleased—you died out. A woman seemed so promising. Here I am, a soft and pretty thing, you can light here with me. And then, one way or another, sooner or later, she transformed into nothing that was light, but instead was a trembling, overly intricate, burdensome . . . *tchotchke*. Who cluttered up your life, who got to wanting things from you that went beyond time and company, wanting solicitude, wanting concern, wanting care. That bright and fragile smile through tears—how it had worn him down. How did the song go? *Get yourself free.*

But these women, the two, so long gone their faces refuse to assemble in his mind. He takes another swallow. What has happened to them?

Has he done harm?

Margo continues on, walks away from her friends with her head high, her shoulders straight. She looks strong. She seems sure of herself. And he's reminded of one of the earliest painful moments of their marriage, when she had asked him to make love to her. He'd been distracted—a new record, was it really as banal as that?—he'd wanted to listen for awhile.

He took his time. She waited in a pretty nightgown. She, so take-charge, even abrasive, became kittenish, almost shy in bed, a detail he'd been happy to acknowledge to himself. A lover's secret. He could smell her perfume. She looked dewy and soft, lying in their big gold and cherry bed, bronzed by light from the hallway.

So why didn't he want her? He undressed and got in bed. They kissed for a while. The magnolia tree outside the window breathed a heavy scent into the room. It mingled with her perfume. It was distracting. He kept wishing to close his eyes and live for a few moments in a purely olfactory world. Finally she turned away from him.

"You know," she said. "I don't think I'm up to this tonight."

His hand was on her shoulder, heavy and warm. "No? Well. Too bad. I thought you wanted to." He thought he should draw a strand of hair behind her ear and touch the taut skin there, and he would do it, in a moment.

But the silence between them became a presence in the room. And he knew the consequences of letting such a silence deepen. So he said, and remembered, now, feeling as though he shouldn't say it, "Did I do something wrong?"

Another thoughtful moment on her part. It's always bothered him, the way she insists on the careful, measured response.

"Well, Ripley, to be honest about it, I don't feel very desirable."

He did touch her then, brushed back that errant strand of hair. But found he could not let his hand linger. "I don't make you feel desirable?"

She was angry. "That's not it, Ripley. *No.* God. It's not about how you can make me feel," she said. "It's about *the way you really feel.* Which is fairly apparent." She rose up on one elbow to thump the pillow, flopped back onto it with energy.

"I don't think you get it. Our whole success here, in bed, has to do with desire and response." She spoke to the dresser beside them. After a moment he moved his hand down over her breasts and placed it just beneath them, pressing gently there.

"What is this, a progress report?" he said. She as teacher: a motif that had provided them moments of pleasure in the past. "I think we've been fairly successful."

Her voice was clear, stronger.

"If by success you mean that I thought we'd learned, you and I, that when a woman is wanted, she responds by making you happy." Then, softer, "Very happy."

He sighed. On another night, perhaps a year or two before, she could have continued. She'd have accepted what he could muster for her at that point. They would go on, and afterward there would be the promise of rest. But on this night she'd surprised him. As he began to speak, she'd shushed him. "Let's go to sleep."

"Let's not yet," he said, suddenly unwilling to cross this line. He kissed her neck, he wanted to now. Now his distance, having been acknowledged, could be weakened, could be ignored by both of them. He moved his hand gently over her body.

"No, really. I think we can do it. I think we can avoid thinking about this long enough to fall asleep." She took his hand and moved it back to where it had been resting on her ribs. After another moment she placed it firmly away from her body, turned from him, and closed her eyes.

Here in the pub, Margo will return at any moment; and if he can make it until that moment, he will not have ruined the evening. He runs his fingers along deep grooves in the glossy table. Rough, shellacked—of a much lower quality than his trestle wood had been.

Great Salt Lake trestle wood was cut mostly of Douglas fir, tight and dense, rosy stringers and pile caps. Straight-grained, just a few whorled, burled knots, even silky; and strong, strong, to carry a freight train. His had been contaminated, of course, with spikes and nails, much of it marred with holes. Distress that made it quite striking once it was de-metaled, beyond lovely. Uniquely cured, with water and salt and water and time and always water. With the sounds and the load the trestles had borne. He should have kept some, had something built, a chair or a mantel; he cannot recall if the wood was fragrant. Of course, there were good reasons to sidestep nostalgia. Still, the wood had been returned, reclaimed. That's what he had done. He'd brought it back. He pictures the tender gradated hues in a pinecone.

He's a little lost in thought when Margo returns. But he stands as she arrives, only partly as a joke; he pours her a little more wine. She smiles and continues talking, a gentle ebb and flow of sound, like the movement of water itself. What does it cost him to listen? He watches her, nods, going along, giving in. Just to try it.

She's telling him a story about when she was a girl. "I was turning six, it was my birthday. And I kept telling my dad I was six, but he'd say, What? No! You're sick?"

"No, no Daddy, I'm SIX."

"Sick? Margo! You shouldn't be up. Do you have a temperature? You'd better get to bed."

She touches the tines of her fork to her lips and shakes her head. "I think we kept that up the whole year, until I was seven."

Had he forgotten this story? Never heard it? He imagines her at six, pictures greenery, dappled shade, a hula hoop. Her fine chestnut hair, her twirling limbs. An innocent creature who never asked to be born, but who wanted so bravely, so audaciously to be a part of the world.

"That's sweet, Margo," he said. You didn't always speak fondly of your dad, he almost said. But thought better of it, why sully this one pure memory?

"It's so silly. I can't believe I remembered that." But she flashes a look of gratitude.

Their failure had been his failure, he supposed. A failure of the very generosity he wanted to embrace now. Who *didn't* want? He saw his mistakes from an elevated spot, looking backward at the stinginess of youth. He felt wiser, even smug—and knew even so that he was foolish to suppose such a stance could be maintained in the face of the day-to-day. *Behavior is consistent over time.*

His own father used to say that. A merchant, owner of a hardware supply, bringing home the reliable odors of camphor, sawdust, and pipe tobacco. Steady, decent, kind. Aging with a slight tremor in his hands before he died courteously, waiting until after the holidays. It had taken the ten years since for Ripley to acknowledge he'd been embarrassed by his father, had privately decided he was a sell-out, a bit of a stick. Hardware, for decades. But perhaps he'd been unfairly reductive.

Maybe, too, he'd not given enough credit to his mother. Both of them gone now. He knocks back a swallow to steady his gaze; tears have unexpectedly needled the backs of his eyelids. He remembers how his mother worked at loving Margo: went out of her way to read books Margo taught so as to know her better. He shakes his head. This had embarrassed him too. He'd been afraid his mother would say something stupid, had, in fact, avoided drawing his mother into conversations that would reveal her ignorance. But what seemed simple and needless on her part now spoke to him of a gentle grace. He was softening. She'd had her influence after all.

He is beginning to see that through the years he has harbored an uneasy, fundamental distrust of life and its offerings. And the world has generally repaid him in the same manner. His marriage had bored him. His businesses had grown stale. Women had tired him. He found it difficult to believe in anything extraordinary or transporting. Religion he had found to be a sham, this was acknowledged even by those in its inner realms. But his parents, always busy with efforts of decency and livability. They seemed valiant to him now.

It was too bad. For when it came down to it he doubted he could change. Revision was for the young. It may well be too late.

For a moment he wonders why anyone keeps trying. Why Margo does, with two marriages besides their own— the ways she manages to reinvent herself, to start again. The fact of her courage presses on him. He shuts his eyes, intent, feeling himself to have been small-minded, picayune, a coward at heart, to a degree even Margo has not guessed. He lets the ache of this knowledge clutch at him. As he looks around, getting his bearings again, it comes to him, such a simple thing: that a lot of people drink too much.

"Anyway. Your theory?"

"Oh, well," she tosses her head, clasps her hands under her chin. "It's just that the stage of rebellion can't be skipped. It's biological. Organic. It's about identity. Better for them to get it out of their system now, than to wake up in fifteen years and throw off a family. Or a mortgage."

She laughs. "The consequences get so much heavier with time. I'd rather they kick their feet against my class, the university system. It's a lot more forgiving. Hell, I'm a lot more forgiving."

"Than what? Than just life? Do you mean to say a mid-life crisis can be averted?" he asks her. "By a sort of . . . coming of age . . . what? Not crisis. More like anger-fest."

She nods absently. "Something like that." She's tired of the topic, or of his questions, perhaps sees flaws in her theory.

He smiles and sends her a look: he was always too slow for her. And there are limits on her desire for analysis. They are heading into dangerous territory. They won't be talking deeply about the crises of advancing age, of encroaching loneliness.

Instead they chat about his latest venture, where he's found "people will respond to a genuine handshake." She listens mildly, more silent now—the alcohol—running her finger around the rim of her glass. She says she needs a break from literature, it's lost its sense of purpose for her, though she supposes this is temporary. She's considering a backpacking trip alone on Vermont's Long Trail. She describes the Gore-Tex jacket she's planning to buy. None of what they say seems important, but the fact of talking itself. That seems important. Margo's eyes are shining—he's read somewhere that eyes hold their youth, never changing.

"Anyway, what's this . . . *maudlin* note I detected in you earlier tonight? Lord. You were so morose. There are worse things than turning fifty-five."

They say it together, laughing. "For instance, not turning fifty-five."

"It's fifty-eight, my love," he says, smiling. Dear, deft Margo. She's offered a free set of years to massage his ego;

perhaps she's tossing away the last busted-up years of their marriage.

"Don't short-change me," he tells her. "I've earned every creak in these old bones."

"Hmmph," she says. "You don't look so bad, for all you've been through. You need to find yourself some sweet thing to take care of you, put you to bed early." She leans in, touches his tie.

"Get married, Ripley. Married men get a lot of sex. Married men get a lot out of . . ." she shrugs, just a little drunk, ". . . marriage. Friendship. Fresh towels. Grapefruit spoons, you know, with the little serrated edge. I bet you don't have those."

He touches her hand, presses her fingers in his. *Leave a party while it's still fun*, his mother had said. Her words swim into his consciousness: they had used to provide excuse. Tonight he sees them differently. The lights are keen and bright, and Margo has made him smile. Regret is something piercing they could maybe leave on the table for a time, slide it beneath a coaster, drop it into a crystal glass. He drops his napkin and stands. Margo looks up at him, her eyes wide.

Ripley bends to kiss her cheek and fingers the corner of his wallet. "I'm going to call you a cab," he says, not unkindly.

She lets the moment pass, sipping the last of her drink. He can see that she will not, after all, pay for the evening, despite his birthday and despite the fact that she called him. It's going on account, against his long litany of dismissals. They have their old reliable games. The milk of human kindness, soured companionably over time. He leaves cash on the table.

With his fingertips on the bills comes again the simple pleasure of doing something for her. It's not the cash, but the gesture of the cash. The fact of the evening, of response, of repose. Margo will be put into a taxi, swing her still-pretty legs up off the curb and be shut, gently, behind a yellow door in the rain, and he'll walk the several blocks home.

As he walks his shoes make a satisfying scritch on the damp sidewalk. Here are the raindrops, pattering on the concrete. Here is the glimmer of the streetlight. There is a new coffee shop across the way, going up. Its promotional sign is understated but softly glowing. He stands looking at the shop. Rain falls a bit harder now, drums onto the shop's empty beams, seasoning them, curing them. The buried railroad trestle in the West. Sad story submerged there, no doubt, someone had lost everything; but then it became discovered treasure. Glory out of wreckage, blunt and clean and without artifice. Retained, as his mother had used to say, *while the customs slept.*

Her words seem wise, elusive, having to do with substance at the core of life, with ideas of recovery and also with his underestimation of her. Hell, of much more than her. If he could dare to believe in such hope, in the wide arms everything finally has. To do for someone. To *feel* you want to do, with no trappings, no hesitations. How could such a thing be so simple in the happiness it brought, and could you hope it might continue? He wants to imagine there is still time for what hope can do.

At last he makes it home. See him now, in bed, dry as tinder, warm, too comfortable. Tomorrow he will continue—come morning he'll acknowledge some shifts in his perceptions. *Gradually, then suddenly*: a literature thing Margo had used to say. The weight of the blanket is tight across his chest, and he can feel it beating on. His heart. Errant and wandering, consumptive—and yet. Also having been built gradually, revived and restored, over decades, from something close to ruin. He waits for sleep, for the irony, the portent in the unvarying rhythm that finally sends him off. Keats. Or possibly not. Possibly Shelley, or one of the others. He finds that he has added to it, and why not? They're dead. Margo would approve. She'd put his words into those little square brackets for him.

"[Don't be] An old, mad, blind, despised and dying king."

. . . . . .

"[You're not] An old, mad, blind, despised and dying king."

The Mandelbrot Set

AT FRIEDLY'S EXCHANGE, residues clung to fingertips and grabbed at the soles of shoes. Tattered books, chipped pottery, a dead man's suit—all less tinged with nostalgia than ruined by desertion. Ginger's parents went thrifting most Saturdays, bent on a course of rescue and appeasement. Malcolm looked for old, odd compasses for his collection; Edie for gardening tools, china, decoupage.

One Saturday Ginger tagged along. She peeled a tiny sock off a music book whose cover was gone. Ribbons of rubber cement leaked from the binding. But there was a promising Table of Contents; and the inside pages were creamy and fresh, notes and staff lines black and substantial.

Home that afternoon, Ginger discovered, in the preface, obscure lyrics from a Goldberg Variation. At the piano, she worked the passage. "It is so long since I've been with you," went the melody, cool and green and staunch. Buried, lost in a swirl of harmonies. She pressed the ache from her shoulders. Time, patience, repetition, belief. She tried again, and again, and finally her fingers lifted the punch line from the keys: "Cabbages and turnips have driven me away."

She's the only daughter of an actuary and a homemaker. Good-hearted, decent people—among the rare Mormons in the Delaware Valley—they showed up for work and kept the house nice. They were devoted to their pretty, earnest daughter. They wanted so clearly, through piano lessons, an orderly home, their new faith, to ensure her successful life.

"Ginger!" Edie called. "Come help with dinner."

Ginger tapped a loose-hinged, responsive ivory key. Chipped, deckle-edged. Imperfect. She took up the song again, relieving the uncertainty she could only escape through pursuit. Time, patience, repetition, belief. Intensity like Ginger's could mask reservation, shyness, turn these into something aloof. She's heard the soft voices of her parents. "People will have to get to know her," said her father. "Not so serious, honey," sighed her mother.

Edie was referring to her daughter's torturous expectations. Where did they come from? Where would they take her? Ginger's sober face held a look of hope and capacity. Other girls become audacious, street-wise. But Ginger could not change the fact that, well, she did not wish to change the facts. What was significant and extraordinary would present itself if she remained patient, attuned for it. The nuanced, the forgotten, insignificant detail. "It is so long since I've been with you." A detail like that could change everything.

Edie walks into the living room, her mouth set in a thin line. She twists a dishcloth; she may just slide the piano lid over Ginger's fingers. But the music stops her. Edie drops into an armchair. She listens. It is so long since I've been with you. . . .

———— /// ————

At Ginger's high school, ordinary details merged in a pleasing mix. Inky dittos, rubber-tipped bottles of glue, the dry residue of chalk in a blackboard tray. A busy hum between classes, the slap-slap sneakers of someone running late. She felt locked in tension, ready to spring—the word for this, picked up in French class, was *couchant*; her senses pulsed with a tight-stretched thrum. Who else felt this way? Not her classmates, loud and breezy with confidence, or gloomy and sad, slipping along the margins with downcast eyes. One afternoon Ginger slipped into a woody, fragrant supply closet. She took a black-and-white theme book from a shelf and opened to a random page. She wrote:

September 22nd, 1962. I have a new lipstick, Tangerine Tango. My bicycle's flat, and Ed Briscoe says he can fix it during lunch. This afternoon Mr. Shumway will demonstrate the solving of oblique triangles. The best ice cream is strawberry, from Delsa's on Kelty Street. If you are reading this, maybe you know me

She added a flourishing exclamation mark. Her shoulders tingled, but how poorly the careful writing expressed this—not what she'd meant at all. She replaced the book with a sigh, eased the door open and joined the channel of students in the hallway.

After school, Ginger worked at Krummerhorn Bakery. It was old-fashioned, with a bell at the door. Swirl-textured, faded red paper covered the walls. Tin lampshades housed bulbs hung on thin cords, spreading circles of light over pastry cases and wooden counters. At the till, Ginger was expert at adding long columns of prices in her head and making change.

As if to add to its nostalgic qualities, two older women worked there. Lorraine was slow-moving, with sad eyes and hair stuffed into a colorless net. She polished the shelves and patched icing in the pastry cases with thumb and forefinger. Betty had black, bouffant hair and nails and lips painted red. She presided at the counter, refilling straws and napkins, making small talk. Betty refused to step into the back room to retrieve trays of cakes and cinnamon buns. Lorraine moved the goods, shuffling across broken linoleum with plastic trays pressed against her concave chest.

Mornings, Fasching the baker plunged his hands into vats of dough and shaped hot cross buns, French bread, Kaiser rolls with sprinkled sugar. He spoke broken English and never wasted a moment, nearly always finished by three o-clock. Ginger had seen him only a few times.

That day, Lorraine telephoned. She wasn't feeling too pert, so Betty pulled a stool to the till. Ginger stacked three spattered trays and backed through the swing-hinged door to get them washed.

Fasching stood in the shadowy corner, drinking from a dented metal cup. Perhaps he'd killed the yeast that morning with hot water, stayed late to remix the dough. Light was poor, and near the sink was a refrigerator. Ginger stood on tiptoe to place her trays on top of the fridge. Her arms rose and her head tilted up, like a dancer.

Freeze her for a moment: soft-limbed, supple and dewy. Her yellow top slid above her jeans, and her Laurel advisor, Sister Connor, came singing into her mind: Raise your arms; if your tummy shows, put them down and go buy new clothes.

Sister Connor was the mother of four genius boys and seemed to have long forgotten what it was to be a young woman. A girl. Who should—approach? invite?— well no, she should simply *be*, in an artless sense, never in a conscious, adjust-your-clothing manner. Anything more is pretense, distraction. Cabbages and turnips. A girl be's simply lovely. To be was enough. The best books and music would agree.

These were the thoughts on the dreamy fringe of Ginger's mind as she placed the trays. Her waist became especially thin; the gap between her denim waistband and her torso widened. She made a sound, a tiny, feminine noise. It seemed to flip a switch in the baker.

Ginger jumped as his cup clattered onto a jumble of knives and shakers. A blur of motion, and Fasching clamped one hand over her mouth. He thrust his other hand into her jeans.

Her body must have been to him the whitest, most tender and fragrant of pastries, and he whispered hot against her ear. A threat, a demand, an assurance. His fingers smashed against her. She kicked at the refrigerator and jabbed his legs with her heels.

Stay miss, now miss, stay miss. Finally his fingers found her, crammed themselves, burning, one at first, then two and even three, inside.

Ginger began silently reciting prime numbers. One, three, five, seven. Eleven, thirteen, seventeen, nineteen. Twenty-three, twenty-nine. Thirty-one. Eleven prime number days each month. Eleven itself a prime number! No, some months had fewer days. Fewer numbers. A spasm of panic, and Fasching tightened his hold. A furious search for a pattern to the numbers—nothing—this lack of design seemed itself enough to make her expire—and then he released her. He clambered to the exit, scattering a stack of pastry boxes. One hand fumbled at the door; the other hand he held to his nose.

In the bathroom, light gave a blurry, silvery sheen, and Ginger's skin was gluey with sweat and fear. She worked her jeans down. Her panties, their dark blue flowers like gravel, or buckshot. The cotton liner was unstained, childish. This brought some relief, but these panties could not be hers; they belonged to the girl who'd yesterday slid them neatly into a drawer. She touched herself, tender, bruised; but her fingers were cool. She pressed, trying for something substantial, restorative in the softness there. Or maybe it was better, more normal, not to find a *there* there.

That night and next day were weathered in a numb shock. Her limbs were heavy. Walking home from school, Ginger saw a mother duck with her chicks tottering behind; yellow down rippling, fragile and bold. Ginger thought of her own mother. She should tell Edie.

Could she have picked up yeast, or worse, from the baker? Could she be pregnant? It might depend on where Fasching's fingers had been. Even if they hadn't been "anywhere," fingers were part of him. Who was to say that ejaculate—a fluid, after all, thin and soapy, if Ginger's friend Daisy was to be believed—who was to say it couldn't migrate? That it wasn't found all through people—through men—even in their fingertips, like blood? As for blood,

Edie'd recommended against tampons. "Darling, let's not try those yet. That's where the man goes, after all."

Edie's words—delicate, courteous—brought both parents to mind. If Ginger told Edie, Edie would tell Malcolm. Something clutched her ribs. Her father called her "Sissy." He came into the living room, rustling his newspaper, when she played piano. Not a demonstrative man, he'd once bought her a collection of show tunes for the piano and left it on her pillow. *Carousel. Oklahoma!* They seemed preposterous now, a cruel joke from someone else's life.

Was this one of those reasons you were supposed to see the bishop?

Was she still a virgin?

These were real questions, but they were nothing against the question of her father's regard. Malcolm, knowing—a certain, needless heartbreak—and whose heart? Hers, or his?

The ducklings made their way into the cold pond, paddling crazily this way and that. The water swirled. She'd carry this knowledge herself. And somehow remain intact. Otherwise, in Malcolm's eyes, something would be broken forever, something that, despite the baker, had not broken yet. Something had happened to her, something awful. Like the monthly gift, ugly and messy. Also private. Adult. To be assimilated, with other adult things.

Ginger said she needed more study time and quit the bakery. Beyond that, the single change anyone might have noticed was she could not endure the smell or taste of soft breads or raised donuts. Puffy, smooth—nauseating. She thought rarely of Fasching as she moved toward graduation the following spring, at Blackhawk stadium. Before the procession, students lined the walls of a concrete tunnel. Morning breezes had wilted, the air already oppressive.

Ginger watched the restlessness of the graduating class. Ahead, a boy with wiry blond hair was wrapped around her friend, Daisy. He kissed her hard like a soldier back from war, and when they staggered apart, Daisy lit a cigarette and leaned against the concrete wall, hooking the toe of her shoe around the boy's ankle. He shrugged her off and stabbed at the asphalt with his sneaker. Daisy pulled so hard ash consumed a third of the cigarette, and she blew a stream of smoke through a jagged sigh, languid and weary beyond tears.

Daisy's drained, heavy-lidded manner seemed to carry Ginger's spirit away from the line, out of the heavy day, back to the burnt-sugar scent of Krummerhorn Bakery. She saw Daisy's motions in the older woman, Betty; saw Betty's refusal to step into the bakery's back room. Watching Daisy, Ginger understood: Betty recognized something, the remnant of a fever, the answer to an old question, in Fasching. She knew what he might do to a girl who'd not known better. Yet Betty let it happen anyway.

Well. Why not you? Ginger could imagine Betty saying, with her chopping laugh. It's time you recognized the way things are.

She, this girl next to her, Daisy up ahead—they were nothing alike. Sister Connor had often shared a scripture about how each girl was fearfully and wonderfully made. Pretty, pretty words that brought Sister Connor to tears. But rather than fearfully and wonderfully, perhaps that verse should say regretfully. Disastrously made. Who'd suspect that Ginger, the only Mormon at the school, took the sacrament each Sunday and wondered, as she dropped the paper cup into the tray, if that meant she could still be a virgin? Rumor held that Diana Bruceton hosted séances on Sundays. For some reason, Michelle Forster never did sleepovers or field trips. It was whispered that Krystal Grinnell ran a prostitution racket, marked by tennis racquets in basement windows. And there was Daisy, who swallowed her mother's tranquilizers at the communion cup. Here in the tunnel beneath the bleachers, the uniform of graduation did even more to equalize them. Easy pickins, however wonderfully made. Or, worse, accomplices to the way things were, to what Betty understood.

Then she remembered the other, listless woman in the bakery. Lorraine, in her hairnet, patting her sunken chest. Ginger saw warning, knowledge there, too, in Lorraine's refusal to tempt the fever of Fasching. Some people had twice the store of fearful as they did wonderful. Was there some ticklish honor, a feather of satisfaction Ginger had taken, in being desirable?

If so, it had only gotten her hurt. Graduates moved through the tunnel now, walked toward who knew what. For a second, she had it back, she stood on the verge, recalled the sensory quiver, the lovely poise—*couchant.* It faded as quickly as it had arrived. Here was the mouth of the tunnel, the edge of shadow and darkness. Ginger stepped forward, emerging to sunlight bright and dim, the kind of light that puts dark shimmering circles before the eyes. The sort of light she had to look around to see through.

——— /// ———

At Rutgers, Ginger studied mathematics. She admired clean, logical processes, the building of one step on another, proving thus and so forth. She'd underlined a phrase in a textbook: *The goal of dynamical systems is to understand the nature of all orbits . . . generally this is an impossible task.* The notion struck her as valiant. Fearful and wonderful. Her pages of proofs, notes on systems and processes; the old musical languages of Bach and Mozart. If design could not be understood, at least there was the attempt, the rare achievement of elegance.

The thought was a stretched, gossamer thread, even a thinning link to the church; but as years ticked by, it was not enough to hold her. Gradually, she stepped away from Mormonism, to the regret of her parents and certainly of Sister Connor. Time, repetition, patience, belief . . . they'd fallen short for Ginger, who now saw impossibility, absurdity rather than hope. Men were likewise disappointments. A graduate student with a sheaf of grievances against family, employers, his mechanic; the coworker taken with her intelligence, but scornful of everyone they knew, including finally, herself.

One evening, a young artist drove her to a secluded pond. Solemn geese stood, heads beneath their wings. As one awoke and stared at them, the artist caressed her shoulder and touched his fingers to her neck, and she shuddered. She recalled the mother duck, her zig-zag ducklings. The darkness that was Fasching.

Home that night, the artist having dropped her at the curb and sped away, Ginger rifled through her music and found the thrift shop book. She played a Chopin prelude, got lost in its deep bass octaves. Then she settled on her couch with a glass of wine. She tore up the young man's phone number and dropped it into the glass.

By her late thirties Ginger edited textbooks for a publishing firm. No real money, but self-respect, a living in a field she'd once found fascinating. Math analysis, differential equations, chaos theory. Love had only become even more dreary. Obsessive and humiliating. The secretary of the county coroner incumbent had seduced a rival candidate, taken him to a motel where a photographer waited in the closet. If we're not lame jokes we're disasters, Ginger thought. Even her elegant Bach inventions seemed contrived, misshapen, products of a merely human mind.

Her reclusiveness may have been connected to the bakery, to old Fasching. Of course this was too simple. So long ago! That girl was full of folly, the fearlessness of youth. She knew better. She reflected on limitation, the certainty that if you slice each pace in half as you cross a room, you'll approach the opposite wall. But you will never reach it.

———— /// ————

The lecture took place downtown on a gray, chilly day. The autumn sky threatened; Ginger had a headache. At home waited her cushy robe; she could almost hear the light clicking of branches, the hush of raindrops against her window. All tempting.

All stale.

She resisted, and went to the lecture. The sound system was faulty, so things were getting off to a slow start. Ginger pulled colored pens and a folder of work from her bag.

A man called Ripley McCord was in the same building for an investment trade show, but had wandered into the wrong room. He knew his mistake but lacked energy to continue with his plans. The predictable contacts, the handshakes. Perhaps here he'd find some diversion.

He squared his shoulders and took in the scene. On a program sheet he caught the word *Fractals*. Grim prospect. But a screen, sweet Lord, something to look at, or to shut your eyes against. The room was nearly full of men. Well, then. Substance. No Mary Kay ladies, no frou-frou, no sniveling about something you couldn't quite name. His ex-wife knew a poem about this, the need of the world of men for me. Look, horn-rimmed eyeglasses, sportcoats. His fingertips twitched. You never knew, he'd once turned a cocktail party remark about conical energy into a cool thirty grand.

And women, some. Some. He ran his tongue over his teeth, trimmed up his gut. Shirt was fresh, from a lunch-hour laundry service, because you never knew.

Two women caught his eye. One held a plastic cup on her palm, listening to someone tall and enamored. She jabbed her ice with a toothpick, lifted it to her lips and plucked off a cherry. Pretty mouth. As she listened, her eyes narrowed like fishhooks. She flicked her gaze over the man's face, a flash of contempt crossing her features. How weary of people and agendas McCord was. Still. *If she turns from him, and those ivory shoulders face my way, I'll go to her.*

The second woman: slender, pretty, not striking. Seated, ankles crossed, she made delicate circles and notes on some papers, quick strokes of her pen. Her bright hair escaped a clip, and she tangled her fingers in it. She touched her pen cap with her tongue.

He'd bypassed these earnest, inward-looking types. They so quickly made him feel his lack. But this woman. Self-contained, calm, unrattled. Near the end of a row, and God love her, the next seat open. *If she touches that pen to her mouth again, I'll go to her.*

Ice Woman, ahh, walking away. Beautiful hips. He turned toward Slender Bookish, and . . . there, pen to her lips. He made his way over, lifting a briefcase and an umbrella.

When he took his seat, *older gentleman* beamed quietly across Ginger's radar. She read and marked a paragraph on Bolyai's geometric intervals. There seemed little progress with the sound system, perhaps the meeting would be canceled.

Then he spoke. "So this is what happens when you've got a roomful of academics and no engineers."

She looked up and gave him a smile, let her eyes linger. His were green with gold flecks. His voice was practiced. Maybe an academic himself.

He settled in his chair, feeling a welcome mix of contentment and challenge.

The lights dimmed at last. An apology and introduction, polite clapping. Then, an Indian mathematician presented a glittering array of slides called the Mandelbrot Set. His

English was barely decipherable, but what he shared was fascinating.

The Set was a perfectly balanced graphic, the illustration of a series of complex numbers resulting from a simple polynomial function. The series long since discovered, but only recently plotted and visualized. Slide after slide showed dazzling paisley-like formations, unseen before the advent of high-speed computers. A murmur filled the room. Ginger realized she'd been part of the reaction. She caught Ripley's eye and smiled again.

"That's so beautiful," he said.

It was. The Mandelbrot Set had a heart-shaped body, curved and sensuous, two small orbs flanking each side. Below the heart, a circle, then a circle smaller still, spilling toward an elongated vee-shape like a birth canal. Mandelbrot was of the class of complex number sets known as fractals, where any cutaway contains endless small copies of the whole. Ginger's mind fired on connections—corona, eclipse, exquisite crystal.

At the next slide, Ripley gasped and felt it necessary to apologize.

"My lord," he said. "Just when you think you've seen it all."

"Yes. I know what you mean."

He had a single thought, cutting through the fervor of the presentation: there was kindness in her voice.

When had he begun to care about kindness?

The speaker moved on—Julia sets, Lorenz attractors, Fatou dust. Light from the images played on Ginger's face and stained her features blue, fuschia, orange-gold. She began an association with scenes from her solitary life. A green Set's luscious heart became a sliced apple, seeds in symmetry on a ceramic plate. A red Mandelbrot, the symbol of her own virginity, velvet chambers within her body.

I will praise thee, the words rose to mind. *For I am fearfully and wonderfully made. Marvelous are thy works.* Sister Connor's scripture seemed perfectly chosen.

Ripley McCord wasn't sure about what he saw, not at all. A lot of brouhaha, a Spirograph onscreen. Theoretical nonsense. He was wrong, and he knew he was wrong; but look at her—lovely, captivated, self-forgetful—again, he thought, probably wrong. No, but he'd ride her interest. He felt that somehow—and not a moment too soon—his shoulders were being dusted off. There seemed to be a search for underlying dignity in him. She made him want to stay and see if it was really there.

When the lights came on, Ginger felt damp and drowsy. She startled herself, nodding abruptly. Embarrassed, she lowered her gaze to McCord's shoes. Thin, supple leather. A glint of gold from threads in his socks. In the lobby, she lingered, bought a book of glossy Mandelbrot images. People laughed, talked, brushed past. McCord stood near the doorway, glancing through an open newspaper.

When she approached, he folded the newspaper and tucked it under his arm. He asked where she was parked. She accepted his offer to share an umbrella, and they set out.

He asked about her work, how long she'd lived in the city. She answered with reserve. He turned as a car sped past, to shield her from the splashing water.

Then: "This chaos theory. What do you know about it?"

"It's about . . . predictability," she answered. "Scientists rely on theories of cause and effect to explain the way things happen."

"Like gravity, causing an apple to break from a tree and fall." He steered her around a puddle.

"Exactly. But some systems don't obey the rules, so to speak. Their behavior can't be predicted."

He chuckled. "That couldn't be a new idea, could it? We were expecting no more than high clouds today. Perhaps a little breeze." The rain, a slight hush over the umbrella, strengthened and fell in juicy drops.

She laughed. "Some people are convinced that if we could predict the weather we'd be a step away from controlling it. But with chaotic systems—no prediction, no control."

Her words mixed with those from the lecture. Butterfly effect, Fatou dust.

Ripley McCord asked, "What do you make of this . . . discovery, this evidence of randomness in the world?"

They'd reached her car. He looked past the cold stem of the umbrella to her eyes.

"As I understand chaos theory," Ginger answered, "it doesn't explain truly random progression. Just that some systems are difficult to predict, based on what's known. They may appear to be random, but really we don't see the underlying causes.

"Yet." She lifted her chin.

"Yet," he repeated. "Such hope in your voice! So is the idea to someday achieve prediction—and then, as you say, control?"

She lowered her eyes. "Some people love to be surprised. The other day"—how easy to talk with him here in the rain, as the light of afternoonn was fading—"I noticed a new establishment, a coffee shop. Opening near my apartment, on Cameron Boulevard." She was conscious of slipping him this information. "And I'd not been aware of it being built."

The shop. He'd stood before it himself, not long ago. He recalled its craftsmanship, its assertion and plenitude. Potential.

"A surprise," she continued. "Never saw it coming, being built on the side of a bank as it is—my own bank." She touched the car and rubbed her thumb and fingers absently.

"It sprung up overnight. Unsettling, you know? Not to read about it in the paper. Or notice it being constructed.

No franchise, nothing with backing. Someone spent a lot of money, perhaps their life savings, on a venture that may very well fail. On the chance . . . " she looked full into his face, "that so many people will want to buy coffee when they go to the bank."

He was retrieving his wallet. "And yet," he said. "On such chances fortunes are made." He fingered a business card. For a moment she thought, Amway. But no—Ripley McCord, this man's name. His company, a securities firm.

"I'd like to help ensure its success by having coffee with you. I hope you'll call me." He pressed the card into her palm. His fingers were warm as hers closed over them. She rummaged for keys. She thanked him quickly and slipped into her car.

———— /// ————

That night Ginger dreamed of Benoit Mandelbrot. He stood before a Bunsen burner, holding a beaker. Into this he poured, then stuffed, the blocky shapes of numbers.

The numbers in the beaker took on meaning. Her birthdate. Her age. Her phone number. A number standing for freckles on her body. A prime number representing hairs on her head. Mandelbrot took a mallet and pounded the numbers in. She watched, amazed the beaker did not shatter. He adjusted the burner's flame.

An image was released—a large glowing jewel—like a genie discharged by a magic lamp. The jewel grew and took the luscious, fertile shape of the Mandelbrot Set.

She woke as the dream broke into fragments; got up and dressed in a light robe. She found her book of Mandelbrot slides, and stepped outside. On the top step, she sat and hugged her knees. The book rested on her thighs, over the thin robe.

Cool, hushed, and irresistible, this night was. The moon rode high in the clean scent of after-rain. A cluster of red leaves hung like a birthmark over the street. Something brilliant flashed—star? Satellite? It reminded her, of what? . . . she had it: the gold thread in Ripley McCord's socks.

Behind windows across the street, people slept. All seemed connected: breeze, sky, people breathing quietly in their beds. The pulse knocked at the base of her throat like a metronome. Such an impossible effort: to stand and turn, step inside, hear the metallic k-dlick of the door behind her. Finish out the night on her own, and wake to the incessancy of another day.

She counted the steps to the sidewalk—sure enough, still eleven—and opened the book. Lingering over the pages, the blooms of fractal color and light, Sister Connor's verse rose again to Ginger's mind. *I will praise thee. For I am fearfully and wonderfully made.*

In the Mandelbrot Set was a glimpse of all she'd longed for. There was intention in the universe. Some semblance of design after all, in an unimagined beauty. An intersection of hope and circumstance settling near that pulse in her throat—no astonishment or fanfare, but more a tiny key turning sweetly in a familiar lock, recovering a door of possibility. *It is so long since I've been with you.* The pieces of her life—pencil marks in the margins of her Chopin nocturnes, the voices of her quiet, aging parents. The sweet patience of Sister Connor. The shape of her wrist bones and fingers, her piano, droplets of rain on her windshield, even the coffee shop under construction, coming to life— all were precisely placed in a pattern of meaning. This pattern had never happened before, could never happen again. As unique as the record of an empire, it had brought her to this exact moment. She'd stepped into the original autumn moonlight, the first best autumn moonlight. The world was not arbitrary.

The man, Ripley McCord, appeared in her mind's eye, perhaps outside his own empty apartment at this very hour. Her stomach dropped with pleasure, a ripple of light, the possibility—up to me—of seeing him again. This was nothing more or less than how people came together. The next step was hers. Might not work out at all—probability held, of course, that it would not. Nonetheless, something unfolded inside her. Crazy, at her age?—but what a triumph!—to move forward in elementary ways, to risk benchmarks of exposure, they could lead only to greater levels. To discover where her boundaries might lie, their limit approaching infinity.

Who'd have predicted his business card—a fragile, transitory collection of fiber and ink—could find its way into her life this very day, this very moment? She stepped inside, walked her dark hallway, knees weak, shoulders aching. Touched the nightstand. Slid her fingers across its smooth surface until they reached—yes—the firm raised edge, the neat square corner. Her pulse quickened, her voice fluttered in a whisper.

The Home Teacher

BISHOP WARNED BROCK HARTMAN ahead of time. "They'll ask for a food order."

He opened a desk drawer and took out a binder filled with requisitions for the storehouse.

"But they have a decent income from the state, and their rent is subsidized. Let's help them figure out how to live on the checks they're already getting."

He penned information onto a page in the binder and rubbed the knuckle of one hand with the thumb of the other. The bishop's private office, down a carpeted hallway from the noisy foyer, was too warm; his face was pale and tired. He scribbled a signature, tore a page from the duplicate beneath, pushed it across the desk.

"I can authorize this one order since they're just starting out with you. But they get almost $2 thousand a month, and we have working families doing fine on that. See if you can help them manage it." He replaced the binder in a drawer.

"Oh, and Brock." The bishop smiled. "Thanks for taking them on." Already his shoulders rose. One burden among the many, lifted. The drawer closed with a satisfying *thock*.

At the close of priesthood meeting, Brock got the new home teaching list, the same except for this addition.

Merton (P) and Sharla (F) Petshot. 62, 64.
504 East 45th Street Trailer K
McAdam, Idaho
208-555-6732

Brock phoned Brother Petshot, who said to call him Mert. That next Saturday, his wife Terra assembled a loaf of banana bread, a container of jam, and a decorative card with their names—Brock's and hers—and phone numbers. Terra wore her summer uniform: denim skirt, sandals, a thin blouse, and Brock wished she'd put some jeans on, more buffer against the toxic incursion of McAdam air.

McAdam had parts that were okay—neighborhoods flanking the river, the new park near the Shiloh Riverside. But the blocks surrounding 45th Street had an undertow of dissolution.

There were much worse places than this. Skid Row. Pain and Wasting, the dreary district east of downtown Vancouver, BC where Brock served his mission thirty years ago, cross-streets Main and Hastings on a city map. McAdam was Pain and Wasting's little sister; a mini Compton, a wannabe Watts. It couldn't compare really, this was after all Idaho; but it was in the running. Mexican drug trade thrived in McAdam, the newspaper's crime log seemed anchored there. Residents none too friendly—skeletal and furtive or inked up, overlarge. The only legal businesses were a decaying Laundromatic, a dismal daycare, and a salvage auto field. Ruts and potholes pitted the parking lots. Chain-link fences were tangled with weeds and fast-food wrappers; rusty washer-dryers sat like sculpture at the edges of trailer parks.

And there was Animal House, a fetid and riotous boarding kennel for dogs. The Hartmans had made use of it once for Loki, the lanky shepherd Terra brought to their marriage. Brock and Jonah left Loki there, first day of the new family's spring vacation. Jonah was Terra's son, who at twelve had become Brock's son too. In the few years since, twin daughters had been born. It was a lot of change in a little time.

Brock could easily recall how Jonah had looked that day at Animal House: bereft and bleak as Loki allowed himself to be led, tail and head drooping, and then locked into a stained, disinfected concrete slab kennel. Loki turned and watched, panting with steadfast submission, as Jonah and Brock turned away.

"He'll be alright," Brock said. "It's just a few days."

He guided Jonah with a hand touched to the boy's back, and Jonah did not look back, though he did not hurry either. They'd walked together to the exit, as staticky Chopin wafted from speakers to counter the bark and whine and stench of a dozen dogs.

The price this twelve-year-old could pay, to have a father in his life, seemed an outsized force of feeling. But it was not a shock. Even now Brock could be stalled in his tracks by the memory of waking one morning, not long after his own tenth birthday, as Richard Hartman stood in the kitchen, making waffles. Stirring raisins into oatmeal.

"Brock-paper-scissors!" His father called from the kitchen. "Brock-and-roll, Brock-concert. You want maple syrup?"

Brock had thought he was dreaming, but the sun said different, a fuzzy, dazzling blotch through the window. Leaves behind the glass shimmered like sequins. His stomach bounced into his throat, his hands literally tingled. Mom emerged from the bedroom across the hall, later than usual; fresh and pretty, happy; he could still see her, smiling in the doorway. After breakfast, she kissed them both before she left for work. Her hand brushed Brock's neck; it lingered on Richard's forearm.

That Sunday, tall and tanned Richard Hartman waved at the neighbors as the family climbed into his car to go to church. He shut the door gently once Brock's mom was seated, walked around to the driver's seat of a car familiar only in that day's memory: pale vinyl interior, brougham top, slender silver gearshift protruding from the steering column like a magic wand. Richard winked at Brock through the rear-view mirror.

When they reached the meetinghouse, he grinned and shook hands with people throughout the chapel. People clapped him on the shoulder, winked at Brock. "Your dad. Looking good, huh?"

Mormons could be great forgivers. And even better at helping to pick up the pieces when somebody, namely your handsome father, walked out again a few months later. The ward rallied round—with attentive home teachers, with Boy Scouts, the dignity of callings, assignments for Brock and his mom; with expectations and steadfast friendship.

His mother even got past things. "Your dad had a way with people," she said, with a few decades of distance. "Richard Hartman had a way with me. I couldn't fight it, even when I tried." She was speaking his name freely, easily. She shook her head, breathed deep. "I so wanted him to change." Her eyes were steady and pale; their blue matched her quilted jacket. She lived comfortably enough on the pension from a long-running state job plus Social Security. Brock's skills as a tax accountant had helped him help her. She had prudent investments, a tidy nest egg, little to worry about. He'd seen to that.

She touched his hand, her fingers dry as paper leaves.

"We didn't fare too badly, did we? I don't expect I'll see Richard again, even on the other side." Her eyes shone as she turned her face to the window. She shivered, almost imperceptibly. "I don't want to."

Brock was as yet unmarried. Untrammeled. *Not a forgiver*, his Mormon soul couldn't help but whisper. It's all the style today, for women to support themselves and their children. Brock's sense, both then and now, was that a man, a real man, would never cause that to happen.

———— /// ————

He parked on the hard-packed mud outside the Petshots' and was happy to see a car beside their trailer. A nice one, given the neighborhood. Next door, at Trailer L, a quartet of skinny mullets sat vaping. Brock walked around the car and took Terra's hand, and she sang out her hello toward the group at Trailer L, but got nothing. They turned back to the Petshots' home and climbed its wooden steps.

Some commotion and barking, some kitchen noise. The door opened, and Mert Petshot stood waiting in the dim light. He stepped aside to let them in.

A fish tank hummed at their left in a greenish flicker. Four metal cages stood on the far side of the room, two over two, blocking light from the window. A shadow moved inside a low, dark cage, and Terra stiffened at the shape and rise of a cleaver; in a moment, they saw it was only the mottled fur of a Boxer, the flash of white at its throat. To its right was a larger, shaggy black Rottweiler. Its paws scraped against the cage as it rolled to its side.

"Beautiful dogs," Terra said. "Are they friendly?"

"If you're a friend," said Mert, and he grinned, exposing small fish-glow teeth. He gestured toward an old sofa.

"We have a pup and a grouchy cat," Terra continued, smoothing her skirt as she sat. She held tight to the ribboned loaf and the jam jar; perched at the edge of the cushion and kept her back straight.

"And our son Jonah, plus twin girls, and with Brock here . . . I have all the wildlife I can handle!" She smiled, and when Mert said nothing, blinked her eyes at Brock.

"Mert," Brock said. "Thanks for inviting us in. We thought we'd get to know you a bit. Have you lived in Idaho long?"

"You the ones I call if I need something?" Mert asked.

"Sure," said Brock.

"Oh!" said Terra, "and we'd like to give you this." She held out her offerings.

"Got a new phone last week," Mert said. "How do I call you?"

"Take this bread my wife made, Mert," Brock said. Mert juggled bread, jar, phone; and the gifts tumbled to the floor, where Brock wondered if they'd be remembered before dogs were let loose to discover them. He tipped forward and picked up the card, showed Mert where to find the phone number.

Seeing Mert ordering his life on the phone, Brock brought up the church schedule—"The Big Three. Sacrament, Sunday school, priesthood meeting"—and they'd be delighted to see him and Sharla there. "You're part of us," he said. "You're part of the ward. Eleven on Sundays, week in week out." Mert didn't look up.

"Three hours tops," Brock kept at it. "And you find you're spiritually nourished, you really do. I'm convinced it helps to keep the Spirit with me. Church makes the whole week better."

Mert continued fingering the phone, as Brock tried again for conversation. A woman emerged from the dark hallway beyond the cages, as though awakened from a dream. Her jeans were fastened with a safety pin and hung loose. She blinked in the light, and pushed the hair out of her eyes.

"Hello," she said. She removed a stack of mail from a chair and sat down. "I'm Sharla Petshot."

Terra stepped toward Sharla and introduced them. She took Sharla's offered hand, limp as a petal. "I'm pleased to meet you."

Brock lifted Sharla's hand too, for a few seconds, lank and cold, and greeted her. "I was just asking your husband about his service in the military," he said.

"Got a pension from the Army," Mert said. "Plus SSI money, but people always grubbing at it. All-holy VA's supposed to help me with my medications. But you don't get paid for an act of God."

Sister Petshot remarked on the lack of food in the house. "We heard of the Wicker program," she said. "But you can't get any products or disinfectant."

She gestured toward the kitchen, where the stove held a cellophane bag of popcorn and a carton of Pop-Tarts. Plastic 7-Eleven cups had toppled across burners and onto the counter.

"It can be tough," said Terra. "What can we do for you?"

"What're we supposed to eat?" Sharla's words overtook her husband's. "A groceries order from the bishop," he was saying. "I won't get pay until the 2nd." More than two weeks away.

Brock leaned forward, touched his fingertips together. "Okay. But how are you doing with your budget? Can we help you plan expenses? Maybe we can find a way to make the money last."

"I have problems," Mert began. "Didn't bishop say? There's a kind of mental illness I got. Pay rent to stay here, sometimes I can't pay. The church helps people like me."

Across the room, the dog scuffled in its cage.

They talked through the particulars of Mert's income, his rent subsidy. "If the church just gives you food, or extra money for rent, that's not helping you," said Brock.

"The church is interested in helping you manage your resources."

Mert fished out his phone again. "I can't work," he said. "I got hurt."

He spoke in declarations and didn't provide details about his injuries. "The pain is impressive," he said.

"I'm sorry to hear that, Mert," Brock said, hands on his thighs. "But due to your service, to your injury, the state makes sure you have an income and some help with your house. Those are your resources. Maybe we can help you make them stretch."

Mert's head dropped. He mumbled softly to himself.

Brock started to press again, about planning. Terra laced her hand inside his elbow and pulled gently.

"What if we just did the one food order for them, Brock? That will help Mert and Sharla make it until payday. And in the meantime, we can help them figure out a budget."

When Mert heard the words "food order for them," he perked up some. Sharla watched the floor and chewed at her lip; she balled up her fist and knocked it on her knee.

Brock stood finally. "If I was to call, get the Relief Society involved," he said, "when could you go to the storehouse?"

Mert looked up. His rheumy eyes found Brock's face. "My dance card ain't that full."

——— /// ———

"Mormon missionaries, no shit!" Clive Monson said. He began a spiky, pot-holed narrative. "My people came across the U. S. great plains. Not a few weeks but what Brother Brigham sent them on with the handcarts. They were sand-bagged . . . made to move to Alberta. My great, great . . . whatever-the-hell grandfather from Bristol, England." He shaded his eyes with his hands; turned left, then right, possibly imitating Columbus. "They read the Books of the Mormons, they helped to settle the Salt Lake Valley. *Then* they came to Cana-dee-I-O." He laughed. "A saying my mama told me. *Jesus left his sandal straps in Salt Lake City.* She learned that when she was a girl, helped her say her *s*."

This happened in Vancouver, decades ago. Young elders Brock Hartman and Scott Clubbersoll—Canadian Club—met Clive in that Pain and Wasting neighborhood, east of downtown. Clive Monson claimed a distant kinship to the apostle, now become the prophet in Salt Lake.

Clive slumped low against a blackened brick building, and his hands shook as he talked. A pigeon—they were everywhere—pecked at his shoelace. When he tried to stand, Brock helped him up, but Clive collapsed, first to his haunches, fingers clutching at the brick. Then a final breakdown onto the pavement.

"Whoa, there," Brock said. "You want to be careful." Canadian Club got on one side of him, Brock on the other, and they helped him stand once more. It didn't take, and he waved them away to crouch again on the ground. Talking had worn him out. His smell followed the elders back to their flat, stayed on Brock's hands and in his clothes.

But Clive showed enough interest to keep those elders coming back to the blackened building where he held court, and back again; as much as anything to wonder how he'd latched onto a couple shiny, clean-cut boys in double-knit Mr. Mac suits. Talking with Clive, who tried to be cheerful but quickly sunk into a silent, pervading doom, felt like slowly peeling the easy, daylight surface away from things, to reveal an abyss for which the young missionaries believed they had a useful, if not the only, ladder.

When Clive wasn't on the street, he squatted in a flat near the gaslight district, and sure they could teach him there, no problem, after his methadone kicked in, next Tuesday. "My day at the clinic, four o'clock."

Clive felt sorry for Americans because they had it backwards—"no on free clinics, yes on the guns."

Canadian Club laughed at that, hands loosely on the belt of his dress slacks. "Unarmed Americans with health care?" he said, with a wink and a grin.

"That's what you call a Canuck," answered Brock.

Clive mentioned that he wanted to work in America someday, "due to the tax structure," and as he looked up to catch their eyes, Brock realized the three were having an actual, back-and-forth conversation. His spirits rose.

Conversation—beyond Club's supervisory directives—had been in short supply.

——— /// ———

On Brock's next visit to the Petshots', he took a ledger book and a Mason jar filled with Terra's chili. Mert took the jar and looked around.

"You want to heat that up before you eat it," Brock suggested. Mert walked into the kitchen and set the jar against the bag of popcorn on the stove.

"Don't know how I'm going to make it til the 2nd," Mert said, as he turned back. "Four days away."

Brock dismissed thoughts of Mert attempting to heat the glass jar rather than empty the chili into a pan. "Here before you know it. What would you say to making a plan for that money, when it comes?"

He broke the neat cardboard band and opened up the ledger, where orderly lists and columns awaited smart, thoughtful accounting entries. He laid it across the top of a pet cage, elbow high.

"You put the rent money here. Then you decide how much you'll need to spend on food. A car payment might be next."

Mert studied his cuticles. "You bring them groceries orders we talked about?" he asked. "That first one already run out."

Brock said they'd get to that later. First came the figuring of SSI checks, groceries, penciled dollar amounts. He and Mert would clear some space among the animals, sit down and get to work, line upon line. Dog food, fish food; heck, they'd get to the blessings of tithing one day. A simple matter: making a plan, executing it.

"Self-reliance," Brock said. "You have to . . . you know, you have to make the choice, work at it every day, and then, you'll see, you get accustomed to the plan. You start to rely on it. You're making a habit."

"Like cigarettes," Mert said. "You know, I just gotta habit."

Brock cracked a grin. "Didn't take long, right?" He clapped Mert lightly on the back. "This habit won't take long either."

But Mert couldn't work up any interest in the ledger. "Didn't your wife want to be here this time?" he asked.

"I figured we had the budget to talk about," Brock said. "She's busy with our girls." He walked to the sofa and sat a few minutes. He watched the dogs and touched his fingertips together, elbows on his knees.

Mert was still standing at the cage, where he fingered the edge of the ledger's vinyl cover. "Make a deal with you. You give me a order for groceries, and I'll write in the numbers."

Right.

"You'll write in the numbers," Brock said finally. "In the ledger? Or here on the food order?"

Mert stared at him. "Sergeant," he said. "I'll write them numbers wherever you say."

———— /// ————

The young elders, Club and Brock, kept happening by the curbside on Wasting, first avoiding the alleyway near the junction with Pain; but then venturing closer and closer, hoping to connect with Clive. Nobody hassled them after a few times. Once a guy named Piefork brought them a bag of oranges, stepped backwards bowing after they finally took the fruit. A bookstore owner on Wasting kept their dusty, everlasting stack of Books of Mormons on her counter, beneath a tented index card labeled *FREE*. The neighborhood barber trimmed them up every three weeks and refused their Canadian dollars: "My good deed to the preachers. Long as you bring it in washed."

Time and persistence were with them; or, as Club said of Clive, "He's ready. He's golden." And in a few weeks, the two elders were meeting Clive Monson at his flat. For portions of each day, Clive worked through scripture in a weak square of sunlight by the window there; sometimes with the missionaries present, more and more on his own. He liked the story of young Alma, changing his life.

"Brother did a shitload of damage," he said. "Fighting against the church, against God himself." He marked the page with his finger and looked up. "He changed, though. He came through, just like you said. He got to have his words in the book." Clive managed a laugh, mind and body clean for the better part of this new day. "The longest chapters! Dude couldn't shut up."

Club didn't miss a beat. "Compelled to share is why. Like us. We need the gospel as much as Alma did."

Clive looked dubious at this, but he seemed attentive as the elders read aloud. He took a turn, he read verses.

For that which ye do send out shall return unto you again, and be restored . . .

Within an hour, the three men had finished with scripture for the day, and Clive gave his first prayer. *Jesus bless for bringing these brothers here.* A clotted cough, an *Amen.* Clive raised his head, turned toward a taped break in the window frame. A flatmate groaned softly in the next room, massaged by the nearness of God or narcotic.

"I'm-a find a road out of this hell," said Clive. "See if I don't."

———— /// ————

Bishop phoned Brock; kind, but firm: "Brother Mert Petshot's called the house a few times, left a message. He and Sharla, asking for a food order," he said. "Have you been able to work with them?"

They talked it through briefly; and the bishop's message was the same: "I really can't authorize continuing with the orders. There's a way to help them help themselves, surely."

Brock was beginning to doubt there was a way, but he made another visit. It was after dark, and the trailer's lights were dim. A filmy dust cloaked the Petshots' car; a cat scuttled beneath the back end and stared out with glowing eyes. When Brock reached the top of the three wooden steps, Mert opened the door wordlessly and stood aside.

Across the room, the ledger remained, untouched, on the dog cage. Brock mentioned the bishop asked him to stop by, see how things were going.

"Things are just not good," Mert told him. "I'm out of money. I don't know. If I had gas in my car, I could stop at the store, if I had money for the store. But I can't even get the gas in my car."

Brock reached for his wallet. "I've got ten dollars here, you can get some gas with this."

Mert fingered the bill.

"That's one piece," he said, "in a puzzle full a holes."

Below the ledger, the dogs shifted, releasing a smell like old lettuce. Fresh sweat from Brock, cigarettes from Mert. A plug of matted black on the carpet stuck to Brock's shoe.

"You wondering why I sometimes run out, ain't you," Mert said.

"Don't know what I can say to that, Mert."

"You thinking *you* would never run out like me." Mert's eyes held steady. "You and your jar a beans. I seen you with your wife. Your pretty-ass car. You ain't about to help."

Brock wanted to leave. He swallowed and coughed, employed his old and unforgotten tricks of distracting the body. He sucked in his stomach. Touched his tongue to the front of his teeth, opened his throat in a closed-mouth yawn.

He knew Mert had been dealt a tough hand. No family to speak of. His circular talk showed he was a brick or two shy upstairs. Add the Army, which—combat or no—might have been terrible, especially for someone like him. Factor in illness, the never-explained injury. Add compelling habits, stir in everyday wearing-out.

Still, no tragedy had unraveled him that Brock could see. He'd not lost something precious, like a child; a country. Not faced down cancer, or explosives, or any real danger in the service. Baseless intuition on Brock's part, he clung to it nonetheless.

Focus on what you do have, his mother's words, chiming into his thoughts. Mert had a sound mind, sound enough. Clothes on straight, buttoned up. Decent car. Expensive dogs, cigarettes, an expertise at wheedling. Income, from all-of-ours truly and other schmucks paying taxes and fast offerings. The fact was, you were looking at a real American life here—with choices.

And Sharla Petshot loved him. Managed him. There she was, moving in the darkness beyond the front room, waiting for Brock to leave and the day to return to it's familiar depressing rhythm, only with more perishables in the fridge.

"Mert," Brock kept at it, trusting in firm but friendly reason. "When I run out, it's a couple factors. One, I quit watching where the money goes. I don't plan, just spend. Easy to do, because on payday, it feels like plenty of money, right?"

Mert was silent. Keep talking he'd have to cave, just to shut his home teacher up.

"Two," Brock said, "something big happens."

"A car repair, a person gets sick. Sharla sometimes doesn't feel so good, right? Happens at my house too."

Mert pulled out his phone, fiddled with it like a shrewd adolescent. Brock's pulse began to rise. He was concentrated on controlling it when Mert looked up. Sister Petshot had appeared. Same languid manner. Same pilly yellow sweatshirt. Lips curled in distaste.

"Tell him, Mert," she said.

"I got problems, and you have to help me," he recited simply. "The reason why I come to your church."

It was the clearest piece of communication that had happened between them.

Brock decided not to remind Mert that he hadn't *been* to church in weeks.

"My last ward? *That* was a good ward. Helped me all the time. They understood. A man like me got problems. I served my country. I belong to your church."

Smart enough. Likely competent. Opinion by me, trained and certified home teacher.

The big dog's toenails scratched at his crate, an underscore.

"I think you can make it til Friday," Brock said. He let himself out.

———*///*———

After Clive's prayer in the flat, they wiped their eyes like little girls. But Clive had a new worry to surmount. When the elders were with him, he felt he could stop using, quit the chase. But what about when they weren't there? *You globetrotters will be reassigned, get your transfer tickets like you do,* he said. *And what will I—*

This hurdle occupied the elders through a few blurred and corkscrew weeks, during which Clive alternately banished and welcomed them, showed up for meetings and then disappeared. They brought a couple members of the branch by, to help Clive make friends. Clive spoke with charm and clarity one day, mumbled and carried the whiff of vomit the next. He tossed his scripture into a dumpster and later fished it out; he succumbed to the needle, and next day withstood his craving another few hours. For an entire day.

"Clive," said Canadian Club, one bleak but opiate-free evening. "We can't be with you every minute. But listen." He opened his book. "'The keeper of the gate is the Holy One of Israel, and he employeth no servant there . . . whoso knocketh, to him will he open.'"

The young elders prayed. They laid hands on Clive's head and blessed him with strength of body, and then with resolve when the body failed; and for when resolve failed, they blessed him with grace.

As he spoke, his fingers tented and lightly placed, Brock thought he felt the tension leave Clive's jumpy skull. He was sure he could sense beneath his fingertips a curious mixture of softening and firming, as Clive's manic mind and body were becalmed. He thought of it for years afterward, how some sort of bad spirit had truly seemed to leave Clive as they prayed a blessing on him—and as both he and Clive believed in that blessing—didn't they? On that cloudy, whip-wind night, they did.

They reached a week where Clive had gone three days without using; they'd been with him almost forty hours, trading sleep. Their white shirts became dingy, creased and sour from watchfulness. Clive was pale, clammy, twitchy, huddled in a blanket one moment, jittery and pacing the next. The elders sat with him on a depleted futon; one or the other followed him to the bathroom, since Clive was terrified of being left alone, even for the clunking, misbehaving toilet. He crouched and huddled in a corner of the curtain-less shower, through the water's turn to cold. Steam and mist faded as Clive's body was pummeled by the shower's icy shards.

The elders bent the rule of companionship. They took turns ferrying filthy blankets, towels, sweatpants, a tattered gray robe to and from the laundromat a few blocks away. Brock bought bleach and detergent at Woolworth, then picked up two plastic-wrapped packages on a whim— twelve straight columns of white socks. Back at the flat, he unwrapped and folded them, glowing artifacts of a tended life. He stacked them on the kitchen counter like dinner rolls, rationed them to one pair per hour. Clive scraped socked hands over his ribs, his thighs, behind his knees, over his temples. When a bloody hole was worn in the cotton, Brock slipped a fresh pair of socks on him and tossed the ruined set onto a pile of trash. Across the room a stack of dirty towels anchored a corner. Books and pamphlets littered the sofa, across the floor. Food wrappers, soda cans, orange peels. The elders took turns gathering it up and hauling it away.

At the end of the afternoon, Brock stood, in creased, overworn and outsized dress pants; he paced the room as Elder Clubersoll read aloud in the low murmur Clive could tolerate. Brock turned to the broken window of Clive's flat, to the pocked, concrete-wall view. A wedge of dark shadow there, a sharp stripe of hard, days' end sunlight.

The view was small, limited; but he knew what lay beyond it. Vancouver, a chilly, gleaming city beneath pregnant clouds, cloaked in chrome and granite, bordered with the lace of a lapping shoreline. He moved closer, got a whiff of pure November cold, a glimpse of heavy sky. He felt a little better and put his face closer to that clean, clear air.

"A sharp and wondrous evening," he heard himself say. Words he never used, but sure enough, they'd come through his own voice. "Smells like it might snow."

Clive lifted his head. He stood unsteadily and walked to the window.

Brock whispered to him hoarsely. "We read about snow today. *Sins red as scarlet, and then . . . as white as snow.*" He paused and touched his fingertips to the sill. "As sifted, drifted, gifted snow." The words seemed to be coming from his mouth, but not through his mind.

Club was behind them, at the table. He looked up from his reading.

Here was the ladder, a glimmer in the darkening day. *Where two or three are gathered in my name, there am I in their midst.* In the silence, the glow from the window, he felt that the Lord Himself had joined them. The scent of winter, a sweet ribbon of cold traveled into the room, a clean fragrance Brock would ever after recall and hope for.

"You don't *need* nothing, Clive." Club picked up the thread. "You don't need us. You got something better. You got the Lord Jesus Christ with you, right now. You go knocking, man. He's there."

"He's there." Clive echoed the words, in a whisper, the first words he'd spoken for hours. He stood at Brock's elbow, watching the narrowing strip of sunlight on the shadow of dusky concrete.

"I think my fever might've broke," he said weakly.

A few—very few—snowflakes found their way into the small wedge of space, drifted onto the windowsill like outsized grains of salt, conferring quietude. Dignity.

Below them, around a corner was the wonderful ratty bookstore; further on, the grimy, hollow alleyway with its oily rainbows. A pink glow began to suffuse the grayness of the sky, and the tiny dots of snow skittered along, rising and falling, skipping and tumbling like children, as the weak sun behind the building held, and held longer. A slice of light, a sliver.

They left the flat just before the light dropped for good. It was Clive's idea. "I want that fresh air all around me," he said. He might have felt well enough to eat. He clutched at the elders' elbows, needing some help to walk; the snow was piercing, the cold an anvil inside his bones. At the diner he chewed part of a waffle and sat, motionless, pained if either elder tried to talk. They heard the faint clackety-clack of a railroad. "People going somewhere," Clive said. He picked up a pitcher of syrup, set it down again. Too tired, almost, to lift his fork. "It's happier than it seems," he said, looking up at the elders' worried faces. "Happier than it looks."

His eyes had lost their glossy, pinned weirdness. His fatigue spoke of a scraping, a hollowing and cleansing rather than the old tamped down, corrosive and chemical depletion. Eventually he managed a grin. "I'm here," he said. "I'm here. Don't mind the cold, I can *feel* it. About to shoot somebody for a cup of coffee, if I had the strength." The elders grinned back. Brock ordered him a hot chocolate.

"I'm here, elders," Clive said again when the train rumbled again in the distance. "I'm going somewhere myself."

—— /// ——

Friday—Mert's payday—came and went. Sunday, no Petshots at church; but the week after, Mert called a couple more times, and once again talked Brock into a food order.

At bishop's request, Brock brought up the idea of a conservator. The state does this for people it deems incompetent, he'd said. A conservator could manage income, distribute the rent, the utilities, any debt.

Brock may have erred, explaining to Mert the incompetent part.

"Hand off my money to somebody, say, you," Mert said. "Then you parcel it out back to me. That makes as much sense as about . . . about a cocktease in a cathouse."

His eyes jumped from Brock to the fish in the clotted aquarium.

"I'm a small fish in a eat-dog world. Always a bigger fish waiting at the next corner. I ain't giving my bishop your mo—" He stopped, and started again. "I won't give your bishop my money. It's my money."

Brock started to speak, and Mert rescued him.

"Save your opinions," he said. "The point is mute."

Lord help him, Brock submerged a smile.

"'S my money."

"I don't want your money," Brock said. "You've earned that money, through your service in the Army. I thank you for that."

Mert's head moved like a bobble toy. Again, Brock told him, if they didn't want a conservator, a *program*, he'd be happy to help with their budget for a month or two, checking in every few days. But the food orders were a thing of the past.

"Think about it," he said, over Mert's protests, as he left. "This could work real well. And only if that other part wasn't successful," he said. "The planning, the care with your spending. Only then would we go the conservator route."

He walked to his car and didn't look back.

——— /// ———

Not long after Clive was baptized, Brock's time in Vancouver was up. He transferred to Victoria, a place permanently shrouded in mist, where he taught three lessons in as many months. No takers; and after that, his mission was over. As the years went by, he connected two or three times with Clive, who as far as he knew, had stayed clean and kept the faith. Clive took a job as a shipping clerk near the Montana border. He married a First Nation woman who had a son. He played church softball. That son would be grown by now. When Brock married Terra, he sent word. He tried not to worry much, at not hearing back. In the manner of men who shared something too large for talk, they'd kept their communications few and far between.

Both had taken their time, come through some trouble. Each had married a woman with a child, a woman who needed them. Brock chose to believe that each had continued as best they knew, with the best lights they had. Sometimes he read through his old missionary journals, to make sure those miraculous days and weeks with Clive were real. Faith, belief . . . he'd found these to be essential, but not so durable. Choices that had to be made daily, that had to be bolstered with prayer, language, memory. With action, and thus, always in danger of faltering. Hope—desire, patience, meeting faith halfway—that was more constant. He hoped Clive was doing well, that he had managed to hold on to the gospel. Club too. But as to the particulars of their continued pathways, he had no information; no answers.

And no answers regarding Mert. He'd stood so many times now on the Petshots' doorstep, paperwork folded beneath a loaf of Terra's bread. He could picture Mert as a kid in junior high, sitting alone at lunch, often with nothing to eat. Slow and befuddled, picked last for everything. Not likely able to read. He saw Mert's teenaged skinny neck and bad teeth, his unwashed hair, his pants too short, his shirt always stained. His mother in bed all day drinking, sleeping. The Army waiting in the future for his warm, twitchy body, another number toward their quota. His father likely missing.

Brock's father had been missing too. That was of course different. He had many other advantages, a fact he was not sure he'd truly considered before this moment.

"Life's damn expensive," Mert said, on Brock's next visit, matter-of-fact. It seemed to be Mert's only answer. Sharla Petshot moved about in the shadows behind him. "I have obligations."

Gambling debts? Brock wondered. Lottery tickets? Too many fast-food dinners out?

"Isn't this an obligation?" Brock waggled the food-order papers at him. "Keeping back some money so you can buy some damn food? So other people don't have to buy it for you?"

He, holding a casserole, clutching his dispensary, benevolent paperwork. His gloomy charity. He was speaking to a closed door now.

———— /// ————

That weekend, Brock worked a full Saturday. He was driving home, going to press some juicy burgers onto the grill, spend the evening on the patio with his three pretty girls, maybe Jonah would even stick around. They'd have a tablecloth, set up on the good part of the concrete. Play games after dinner. He'd read *Are You My Mother?* with the twins. "The snort went up. It went up, up, up . . . And up went the baby bird." The girls would lift their arms with the words, get tired of it long before Brock would.

Mert called just as Brock made the turn in to his own neighborhood. Surprise, he couldn't make the rent.

"You gotta help me." The dashboard amplified his wheeze. "You're not helping me."

"Are you ready to figure out the conservator?"

"Conservative my butt," Mert growled. "I'm calling your bishop."

"Bishop will tell you the same thing I'm telling you."

"I'm calling him. You won't help me."

Brock eased up on the gas, there were kids around. You could tell the high water bills: Rookers' house, on the left, then the Siddoways', with the chevron pavers. A curve in the road, and his own place up ahead. The lawn needed tending, heat had got to the flowers; but it looked pretty good. For a minute, he was eight, sweaty and proud, come in after cutting their scrabbled patch of grass his first time. His mom was at the stove. Brock looked into the saucepan. Orange fat in broken triangles over the surface of Bar S franks-n-beans. "I'm going to call the bishop," she was saying. Heat filmed up the sides of the pan. "I bet we can have our new home teacher baptize you."

"You do that, Mert," Brock sighed, "Go ahead, call him."

"Since *you're* not helping me," the dashboard accused. "Worst home teacher, I never had. That's all I'm saying."

"I hear what you're saying. I've tried to help you."

Cursing crackled through the dash. *Don't hang up*, Brock Hartman thought. End the call, but don't hang up on him.

"Mert—I have to say—"

"Don't preach to me. Some home teacher. You're supposed to help—"

Brock sped the car. "Conversation's over," he said, and pressed the hang-up button.

He rattled too hard into the driveway, where pink tricycles were flung in a jumble on the asphalt. Daddy was home. They were cooking out.

Last time Richard Hartman disappeared, Brock had been nearly twelve. So when the time came, Brother Thueson ordained him a deacon. He tagged along with Cleverlys on that year's father-and-son campout, and only once. Brock worked the warehouse three nights a week during high school, some double shifts during summer. He kept the job going an extra year. When he put in his mission papers, he had almost $4K, not half what was needed; the church had to help Mom with the rest.

He was at a bad angle, but he cut the ignition and listened to the engine tick. A blonde pixie stood in the picture window, scratching her tummy under her t-shirt. She was holding a six-inch plastic horse, a look on her face like *This My Little Pony has gotten somewhat dingy, Dad.* Brock waved at her, rolled down the window to breathe. His daughter stroked the worn-out silvery mane on her pony. He watched as she looked away, up toward some tree leaves, and sucked her thumb. Terra had painted some foul-tasting stuff on his daughter's thumbnail, but she couldn't seem to stop.

A metallic ring from the dashboard. It rang and rang. Just past the hood, a small bird fluttered up, tracing a crooked path beyond the roofline.

Mack and Natalie Have Gotten Very Comfortable in Idaho

[with thanks to Charles Baxter]

MACK'S NEW ATLAS was gilt-edged, cloth-bound and hand-sewn; two-hundred thick pages—must have cost a fortune.

"So pretty," Natalie said, "the colors intense, like Japanese wood block prints."

What he needed was not an atlas but a new truck. They'd been saving up, keeping the old one running.

The two sat at the dining table, in evening light. She rubbed his calf with her stockinged foot. The house was quiet. Mack turned the page to an orange peel of the globe.

"Did I ever mention," he said, "how world maps in Asia are Sino-centric? China on the left, Japan. The Pacific down the middle."

"That makes sense," she said. "You see the world from your own perspective."

Mack had seen the world in Japan. He'd taken the bullet train, the Shinkansen, across the prefectures. He said that Japanese were formal, eager, on the same team. Homogenous. Team Japan.

He'd lived in Germany too, until his money ran out. Bused tables for a week and scythed a Bavarian wheatfield for train fare. He'd stood at the Berlin Wall, when they still had that.

"Let's see," he was saying. His finger traveled over the page. "South America. Paraguay."

"Wellspring's doing a community water system, just southeast of Asuncion," he said.

"Tell me again about Wellspring."

Mack sat back and crossed his ankle over his knee. "It's that not-for-profit K— works for. Water systems in third-world countries."

Natalie bit her lip. "Is something up?"

Mack picked at his jeans. "Maybe. I could probably do this project. It's a design I know."

She bent over the map. "Near Asuncion." Some fabric behind her eyes seemed to loosen. "So, you bought this atlas. Why, exactly?"

He exhaled. "I just thought."

"Mack. Do they pay you to design the system?"

"Sure, honey. But . . . on-site. They need someone to oversee construction too. They can't pay much."

He stood and lay his hands on her shoulders. There was heat in his touch.

"Pay's in the experience, the chance to do something that matters. Wouldn't it be unforgettable? If it goes well, there'll be other projects."

"Oh good," she said. "Nice atlas."

His hands moved away. "I'd like to come straight out and tell you something, but you make me feel like a sneak."

She sat back. Jory was running cross-country. Ethan, their loner, had joined Chess Club. Michael was learning to read. Evenings, they did the *Just So Stories*, and she bought stuffed miniature animals, one-by-one, to go with.

"It's pretty sneaky. Bring home these maps, like we'll be taking a vacation. Mack, let's not change the subject. You think we could move down there, and sell the house? Home-school the kids?"

"Never mind. I might have guessed."

She felt a ringing in her ears. It was Michael's childhood—the kid she was going to do right by, the one they'd planned for, been able to actually afford—his childhood, shoved aside for some tubercular third-world pipedream.

And then, selfish, pure and straight. She couldn't even object on her own terms. It had always to do with the kids.

She had no idea if *she* would want this venture. She was furious with Mack's certainty about himself.

Her legs felt like paper ribbons.

"Mack, this—your heart, ambition, whatever. I'll be the heartless one, the practical one. It's too big for me. A poor country, the politics probably a mess. We have a family, a whole situation here."

He rested his fingertips on the map. She spoke to the floor. "The kids are doing well. Let's not mess things up for them."

Stupid. As though they'd go if the kids were doing badly.

"*You* go. And come home for a long weekend every few months. Right?" She caught his eye. How annoying to again find his eyes beautiful. But she had to look away, because she'd been bluffing. She knew it, and knew he did too.

Before long she heard the clank of a wrench, the soft clatter of wood and metal in the garage. Sometime later, she went out there and touched him, kissed his brow.

"Come to bed?"

"Soon."

In the night, he slipped in behind her. His heavy warmth, an embrace, familiar and solid, bedrock. Maybe she was dreaming.

Next morning Mack had a trip to a faraway drill site, ten days with a crew; no service. He stood trimming his beard at the mirror. Natalie was behind him in the glass, getting ready for a shower. Mack kept stepping slyly to the right and she hopped along behind him, pulling off her socks.

"Hold still, Mack!" How she hated an unexpected mirror. Too late, she looked up to see something hard come into his eyes.

"A lot of folks are right where they should be." Soap foam flecked his lips. "Me, for instance."

"Something about hearing you say that breaks my heart," she said, stepping into the shower. She could hear him rinsing. He'd take a moment to enjoy the cold water, to cup it over his beard, his closed eyes—he was often so easily, so wonderfully pleased.

She wanted to call out, to have him leave with a proper goodbye, ten days is ten days, but she couldn't do it.

Dressed and made up, she walked to the living room; picked up the newspaper, Ethan's socks, a coffee cup. Very casually she glanced out the window to check the weather, to make sure—yes, he did it, oh *shit*—he had in fact driven away. No lovemaking last night, their protective charm, a vaccination. No kiss. She turned to the most necessary tasks of the day.

———— /// ————

On the last night he was away, Natalie sat in the captain's chair, paging through the atlas.

They'd purchased this dining set from a widowed grandmother. Beautiful walnut, three leaves, chairs Natalie re-covered herself. She'd asked if there weren't two armrest-ed captain chairs, like dining sets in showrooms. "Sugar," the woman explained, "back in those days they was only one captain."

Captain Mack. A tiny flower deep inside her pelvis burst, a little sweet explosion.

He'd owned a motorcycle in college, a tinny Yamaha, whose engine always brought off in her a sexual whirr. He sold it when Jonah was born. The buyer—a kid—came up short, and Mack released the bike anyway. He said: drop by with the money when you can, I'll hold the title until then.

Well. He never got that money—she'd seen the title, still in its folder—and wouldn't bring it up even for nostalgia's sake. Mack didn't like to look back.

He looked forward, altered by events and choices, but never sidelined. Not jealous or suspicious, he was one straight shooter. She'd never known anybody less haunted. But Paraguay was to say he wasn't satisfied with what had become of his life. Their life. A tightness gathered above her eyes.

Was she satisfied herself?

Dangerous question.

She'd arrived someplace comfortable, yet fearful. Slow-moving, quiescent—the center of a pond, where things are calm, but not much is happening. There was a term for this, Mack had used it once, helping one of the boys with his homework. What was it, now? She had it—*a low-energy depositional environment.* Lord. That was her.

Light softened of its own accord. The moon outside disappeared behind some high, scudding clouds—the same moon Mack could see. Such a bloom of tenderness she felt. He'd been so steady, so decent. She'd overlooked him.

She traced a red line on the cover of the atlas. Next day he'd be driving home.

——— /// ———

On his way home, Mack's truck finally failed. A well-loved pick-up with some crazy number of miles; finally expired, just east of town.

He worked a salvage deal with a towing company and phoned Natalie to come get him. Dusk was coming down. She waved as she passed him and parked ahead on the gravel shoulder.

"Hey, honey," he said, as she walked back. He kissed her, absurdly nonchalant. "Timing chain I think."

"Can it be fixed?"

"Not worth the trouble." He pulled a duffle and a hard hat out of the back and clapped his hand on the hood. She wasn't even sure he'd cleaned out the glove box.

"Lucky most of the equipment had to stay at the well. I'm going back next week."

"Driving something better, I guess." She smiled. "Maybe something new."

"Nothing new. But an engine with more kick to it. That'd be nice."

Natalie touched his waist and they walked to the car. Michael was inside, stringing transformers across the seats.

"Dad," he said when Mack opened the door. "Want a sip of my soda?"

"Sure." Mack took a swallow from the can. "What have you got that's good for a laugh?"

"I don't know," said Michael, adjusting a transformer arm. He grinned and lifted his eyebrows, a flicker of light skittering across his face. "There's this one about Helen Keller."

"Yeah? Not the one where she answered the iron. I've heard that one."

"No, Dad, it's another one."

"Let's have it."

"What's Helen Keller's favorite color?"

"I give up. What?"

"Corduroy."

"Ha!"

They took the off-ramp and swung around to the West. Soft conversation. Spectacular sky. Mack's fingers laced with Natalie's on the console. Working car. First world. Home.

So lovely and insufficient.

The Hardness of Steel

This is an industry given to talk of the pouring of steel as both the grandest of games and a patriotic duty.

—Edmund Faltermayer, *Fortune Magazine*

"... AND THE NAME'S JACK." That's the voice of my three-year old. He speaks to the front room, which is empty of people, so I take my coffee and newspaper and sit with him. Jack rocks on his heels and bangs his skinny butt against the cushions of a low sofa that fronts the wide picture window. He's wearing corduroy pants and hiking boots, a brown turtleneck.

Hello, Jack.

It's not familiar to him, this old house we've come back to in Charleroi. My folks are gone, but I see the lines of their bodies in the way Jack's hands are clasped behind his back, in the wiry density of his trunk and limbs. In the right light—not so common in this part of Pennsylvania— his butterscotch hair, cropped close, a little curly, gives off sparkles like a swimmer's; he gets that from my wife.

I'm not sure what prompts Jack to announce himself the way he does, just as I don't understand why he asks me for the time, something he does at five or six various moments every day. I suppose he's trying to claim his bearings. " . . . and the name's—still?—Jack." Like a guy striding up to a counter, affirming his request. Jack knows his world has been upended. We may move back here for a time; we're thinking about it. There are decisions to be made about this house. Jack won't remember his grandpa, who died when my wife was expecting him, and he'll little remember my mother, gone nearly a year. The brush of her hand, maybe, or the way she smelled, powdery and milky together. She had an ease about her, an accommodating softness. She liked the sober bustle of Pittsburgh, the crooked hillside staircases, still serviceable. The hard yet open faces of people, their workaday, understated pride. If she had private sadnesses—and doesn't everybody?—she shielded them from me. And probably from my father. He was a man who inspired restraint.

At some point she has had the house repainted; the odor of my father's Winstons is undetectable to me. But the rest of our house seems unchanged, preserved in a low light, in something like amber. It's Sunday. Forlorn leaves scutter down the steps, though it is the beginning of spring. It's a day for traveling back.

Charleroi, Pennsylvania was a small town when I was growing up, and it's surely smaller now. On the Monongahela River, a little south of the city. My father was one of the few men living here who had been to college. He was the first Jack McGuffey, and he taught economics at Jefferson High School up near Clairton. My father wore a white shirt and tie to work, and in his shirt pocket he always kept a pack of Winston cigarettes and a pair of silver-clipped mechanical pencils. He had a quick, slender build and dark gray eyes, the same as me. He was quiet and had a humble authority. People respected him.

Many of my friends had fathers who worked for Allenport Steel, blasting iron or pouring ingots at the plant by the river. Denny Cholovich lived next door, and he was one of those laborers—a millwright, and a union man. This was not so far back, when a blue-collar job bought a white-collar lifestyle. A kid would start in the steel mills right out of high school because his father and his grandfather had done that and made out well for themselves. The steelworkers' unions were strong, run by a man named I. W. Abel, a man Denny said "took no prisoners." Denny was a big man with a red face who had a new Buick and a new family and plans to take them to Rehoboth Beach for the summer. He liked to talk.

Denny was stepfather to my friend Jim Derowicz. Jim's real dad was not living then. We were in the sixth grade when he had his heart attack at a hockey game. At the time I'm speaking of, Mrs. Cholovich had not been married to Denny very long, probably not yet a year. Our families—the one old and steady, the other fragile and tentative—were brokering a new friendship. They'd come over once to watch the Super Bowl and perhaps another time to shoot pool, and my father had stood in Denny's driveway to accept a beer and run his hands over the silver lines of the Buick.

Mrs. Cholovich did hair in the cellar of their house. When Jim answered their door, I could usually smell the pungent permanent wave solution—perm juice, Jim called it. I could smell it that afternoon as I stood on Jim's front step. I asked him if some nice ladies had come over for their sperm juice. He grinned and told me to shut up, and I called into the house to Mrs. C. to show Jim that she hadn't heard me.

She answered back from downstairs with a cheery, "Hello, Conrad. You boys going out to play for awhile?"

"Yes, ma'am," I said. I stabbed at their foyer rug with the toe of my sneaker and smiled. I winked at Jim and asked him if he had his yo-yo. He grabbed a package from behind the recliner and stuffed it in his jacket.

113

I always told my mother I was going to shag flies with Jim, or skateboard, or bust railroad ties. At my house you had to be productive, in everything from homework to coughing. But we were fourteen and wanted nothing more than to be hassle-free. I knew what was in Jim's jacket: Denny's three-month-old *Playboy*. I'd crammed a couple of Pepsis in my jacket pocket, sure that a pilfered Iron City beer would be missed.

We took off for the railroad tunnel a couple of blocks east of the grade school. The tracks curved under the tunnel and around by the river, with grassy hillocks on either side. The concrete over the tunnel was cracked and graveled. It had long ago been a road. This was a dry, cloudy day where spring had stumbled back a step. The trees had pale green buds and there was a little wind. My mother always watched for the first robin in our backyard, and it had not appeared yet.

"He's all, like, wanting to pipe some tunes in there," Jim complained, throwing rocks into the train tunnel. Denny had partitioned off a part of their cellar for a workout room.

"So," I said. "What's your beef with that?" I didn't think a workout room sounded like a bad thing. Jim didn't answer, and I knew he was in a funk again. I guessed it had something to do with having a man living in your house who was not your father but was trying, however nicely and well, to make it up to you.

I was on my stomach in the grass, looking at Misty Chantelle, playmate from Kentucky. I'd memorized Misty, and frankly, after three months, she and I had grown tired of one another. The glossy paper was creased and wrinkled. Misty's smile looked cheesy, patronizing. I closed the magazine and tossed it up onto the tracks.

"Watch it!" Jim said. "Denny'll have my ass in a sling."

"He'll probably buy you a subscription," I said. The thought made the differences between Denny and my father even more apparent. It had begun to seem to me that my father was too upright and respectable. He was a serious man, interested in things like billiards and union activities. He read newspapers each evening. He coached track and golf, clean and solitary sports. I wished he could coach football.

I said, "What's in the workout room?"

"Weights, mostly. Denny got someone to make them for him at the plant. Stainless steel. *Bee-you-tee-ful.* As Denny says." Jim sighed and flopped down on the grass next to me. "I'm not touching them."

I looked over at him. Maybe Denny was trying too hard. I could see my challenge, heisting Jim up and out of his mood. I scooted across the grass to the tracks and grabbed the magazine, which was flapping in the breeze, and set it on his jacket beside him. He looked out over the greening-up hills and rested his hand on the magazine as he leaned back.

His arm was skinny and hard, like my arms. I opened my fist a time or two and thought about using Jim's new weights. It didn't seem bad at all. Things were happening to my shoulders and arms, and I was newly aware of the fit of my t-shirts. My arms weren't any bigger, really, just more dense, more there. I thought that if a girl looked at them, she would like them. She would like the tight, ropy feel of my bicep, a steel cable, thin-skinned, like the twisted steel cords on bridges all over Pittsburgh. Well-hung, I thought to myself, though I was not sure what that meant. I'm sure I'd have known, if Jim or I had read the *Playboys*, but we had not yet done that. We just studied the girls. The women. It was more than enough. Reading the articles, the letters, the commentary felt like something we would not want to do, something you just know you're not ready for. Right then I was picturing the well-hung bridge north of us, on Route 51 into Elizabeth—its steel girders and the easy sway of its cables. I got up and climbed the broken concrete to the top of the underpass and centered myself over the tunnel.

"Captain America!" I hollered, posing with my arms curled and pumped in front of my chest. "Captain America and his sidekick, Mr. Universe!" I pointed my finger at Jim and gyrated my hips like Travolta. Jim cast his eyes up at me a moment and walked over to the tracks. He started throwing small rocks, and I dodged them, attempting a little hustle on the graveled concrete. I could see Jim's mood lifting. I went for a little more.

"Misty!" I shouted across the hills, flinging my arms wide, aiming for Kentucky. "Misty Chantelle, ma belle! I'm a steel factory, Misty! I manufacture sperm juice!"

Jim laughed, pitching rocks double time, and I shot some chunks of gravel back toward him and watched as they tumbled on the windblown grass. The sun dropped slowly, and the sky washed a pale orange. We could see our breath. Our voices were staccato in the frosty air, the softness of the day wearing thin and clear.

To the east, I could just make out the slow crawl of a river barge loaded with coking coal. I wanted to hold the moment, to stay there awhile longer, but family dinners and homework were waiting. We headed toward the streetlights of our neighborhood.

I remember we played an old game we had devised, where one of us would snap fingers twice and slap fist into palm in that way kids do, the way that sounds like a horse's gallop. At that signal, we were to footrace to the next telephone pole. Jim gave the signal. I can't remember which of us got there first.

——— /// ———

Later that evening, my father sat at our kitchen table while my mother cleaned up dinner. She stood at the sink, taking her time with the dishes. He liked to have a cigarette and talk with her while she did that.

He pushed his chair back and crossed his ankle on his knee. He still wore his white shirt, but he'd taken the tie off. I sat across from him, against the wall, hunched over my geometry book.

"We're in trouble, Kitty," he said. "Allegheny Power and Light bought the steel for the new hydroelectric plant." He tapped at the newspaper, up in front of his chest. "They bought eighteen thousand tons." Or some such crazy amount. The number was so large it had no meaning for me, and I refused to be impressed. My father sighed. "From Japan."

My mother turned around slowly. I watched her face in the kitchen's glow. The windows were dark, and our kitchen felt warm. Her cheeks and the tip of her nose were pink. She was a trim, dark-haired woman, a real lady, my father often said.

"Japan." She dried her hands on a blue towel and pressed them to her face. "Oh, Jack." She paused. "We make it right here, and they're getting it from Japan. What'll happen to this town?"

"Damned union's stabbed itself right in the back." My father lit another cigarette.

My mother turned back to the sink. "Maybe one building project doesn't mean so much. Eighteen thousand tons, did you say? That's like a couple of battleships, is all." But watching her back, I did not think she believed that.

"Ten-week vacations, like a summer off from school. Raises damn near every quarter." I had not often seen my father's neck as tight as I saw it was now. He looked tired, all of a sudden.

"Union squeezes and squeezes until, finally, the imports get their chance." My father took off his glasses and pressed his fingers to his eyebrows. "Kitty, I think steel's dried up. The plants are going to close. Youngstown's already down."

I'd heard my father talk about Youngstown before. It was a town, he said, famous for two things. One, being run by the Mob; and two, having the worst drinking water this side of the Mississippi. I gave a laugh, a quick derisive bark, garnering a brief glance from my father.

My mother poured herself some coffee and stepped to the table to refill his cup. "It's good Barbara has her beauty shop, just in case," she said. "I was thinking of having her give me a color rinse. I'm starting to notice the gray." She sat down and wrapped her hands around her cup.

"Right the hell in our own backyard," my father said. "And the Japanese can get it here cheaper."

He drank his coffee and looked over at her a moment, with an expression I have since come to recognize. It was the look of a man who does not want to miss his cue. He put his hand over my mother's. "I think your hair is fine," he said, kindly. "Barbara does it? Next door?"

My mother raised her eyebrows at him and nodded, a little smile playing on her lips. He said, "I never knew that."

She slid her eyes over to me and back to him, and he turned to help me with my geometry proofs. We got through the work quickly, as we always did when he explained things. When we finished up he lit another cigarette. I stacked my books, stuffed them into a knapsack.

And I remember two distinct though inarticulate thoughts. First, about Jim's mom next door, the way her house always smelled of beauty shop—the thick sweet odor of manicure products, and I've mentioned the perm juice. Jim always carried a slight remnant of these smells on his clothing. I was almost jealous of the delicate odors he was continually exposed to, thinking they—and the *Playboys* too—somehow gave him a degree of privilege into the mysteries of the female psyche that were beginning to plague me. Even today, years later, when my wife does something as simple as polish her fingernails—a thing she does at least partly to please me—the fragrance of the colored jars she uses puts me in mind of the forging of steel and the way it collapsed, the big plants shutting down, one after another, just as my father said they would. How could it be possible my father did not know Jim's mother fixed hair and ran a beauty shop? This was a gap in his knowledge I could not account for. I realized my father had probably never been inside our neighbors' house. The thought made our friendship with their family seem uneven.

My other thought was not something I could put words to at the time. But I felt, still, somehow, that my father, while missing simple facts about the neighbors, was at the same time too smart for what went on around him. It was not the first time I thought that. He had to have felt frustrated because he could see stupidity, like in the unions, and he could not repair it. I knew my father believed in the power of the individual. He was not one for collective bargaining or organizing. He would say people should work hard, play ball, handle their own troubles. In this belief, he seemed nearly alone among the people I knew, and something ached in my chest at that thought. What was happening with the mills was bigger than any individual, and bigger than all the steelworkers put together, and it was bigger than my father and his smartness. Maybe fixing trouble of that size took a different kind of thinking, a kind he didn't have. I wondered if anyone had that kind, and if they did, was it anyone I knew, and what would they do in this situation?

———— /// ————

The feeling in our house that night had gotten heavy and low. I went to my room to listen to some music and get away from union talk. As I walked down the hall, I could hear the placid murmur of my parents' voices in the kitchen, and I pushed away thoughts of lay-offs and closures and just pretended they were talking about something else—my new cousin, just born, whom I'd not seen yet, or my father's track season, which would soon begin.

I stacked David Bowie and Todd Rundgren on the turntable and lay on my bed to watch the ceiling and sip a Pepsi. I wondered if we'd go driving again on Saturday. My father had been putting me behind the wheel for several weeks, in the parking lot at St. Louise and lately out on lonesome highways. It wasn't hard to get our big Ford wagon fishtailing, especially when the back was not full of clubs for the golf team. In February I had managed to scoot the wheels past the thin right shoulder and partway up the dirt hill flanking Braddock Road. Trees seemed to slide in front of the headlights. My stomach swung in panic, but my father said, quietly, to "ease her back on the road, son. Ease her back down." And somehow the tires slipped back onto the blacktop, front, then back, *tha-dunk, tha-dunk*, and my father complimented me on my nerves. "Elegance in turmoil," he'd said. Like proving a geometry theorem.

I straightened my arm above my head to pour an elegant stream of Pepsi straight to the back of my throat. With concentration and complete stillness—those tight arms—this could happen, but it wasn't easy to achieve. The soda dripped down my chin and formed a pool at the base of my neck. I thought of going back to the kitchen and hunting up a straw, but I didn't want to hear the steel talk again. What I wanted was to think of nothing, but when that's what you try to do, the thing you're trying to not think of leaks right back in.

Thoughts of unions and steel mills led to thoughts about the neighbors. I began to wonder about Denny Cholovich teaching Jim to drive, what that would be like. Once Denny had laughed at Jim and me shooting spit wads through straws, and he took hold of the straw in Jim's mouth and tipped it up just a bit so the spit wad would make a perfect arc into the big German stein on the table. Jim twisted away when Denny did that. I thought that if Jim veered off the road a bit in Denny's Buick, that Denny would reach over and right the wheel himself.

At the table that day of the spit wads there had been a tick or two of stillness, and then Denny said this: "I seen a lot of times. And I been a lot of places." He grinned. I laughed because I was so certain, aware even then of the judgment in it, that this was nowhere near true. He winked at me. "You always come back to Iron City."

Did Denny know, yet, that steel was going down? I was sure my father was right. My father was respectable, pre-dictable—hell, boring. But right.

———— /// ————

After awhile the doorbell rang, and I heard my father's measured step. Denny was on the porch outside, and then I heard the door close, and he was in our house. The voices of Denny and my father were rhythmic—*punctual* was the word that came to mind—and I could have drifted to sleep there, with that low backdrop thrumming beneath the music.

But what I did was not that. I turned the volume down a notch and cracked open my door and watched their shadows move, listening to what I could from my bedroom.

Denny was chuckling a bit, too loudly I thought, and he was saying, "—and I never knew how the hell much a kid needs."

My father said nothing.

Denny said, "Barbara's crazy over this. She says we can't live for long on the severance. On the unemployment." His voice sounded slow, expanded somehow, though the words were clear.

"I know steel," he continued. "I'm right there when the furnace swings down, right the hell there to sample the heat. I'm the guy"—here, he paused, and I imagined his finger jabbing at his chest, his face almost in my father's face—"the man, best game in town for open-hearth work. My hands are fucking made of asbestos."

My father, still in his white shirt with the sleeves rolled up, said, "You've been drinking." He seemed to be speaking to the floor. I could picture him standing there with his head down and his hands loosely on his hips.

Denny didn't seem to hear. "This would've never happened at Duquesne Works. Damn union takes decent care of a steel man up there."

My father must have looked up at Denny, who was taller by at least a head. His words were short. "Union's what got you into this mess, is all I can see." But he backed off immediately.

"You'll find something, Denny. You're a young guy, you're motivated. You've got a family to feed. You'll get it done." Hopeful words, but I knew this tone; it was empty, it was placating, it carried a condescension both rare and familiar, and it could make my mother turn and leave a room. Listening to my father, I did not believe for a moment that Denny would find anything.

"Yeah," Denny said. "I'll find something."

I heard the sound of fist slapping palm, and I could feel his restless energy as it traveled down the hallway. "I hear oil's getting big, down in Texas. How about that, huh? Think I could be an Oilers man?" He laughed, short and harsh.

"I think you could," my father said, calmly. "I think—"

"Just don't know what I'm going to tell my mother," he said. "She's lived up there in Duquesne forever. It was tough on her when I married Barb and moved down here. Depends on me, you know. She's good people—good people up there in Duquesne. I can't just leave."

"No, you can't just do that," my father agreed.

It was quiet for a moment. I waited for my father to say something perfect, the way everyone in that house wanted him to do, and expected he would do. Clearly Denny had come to get some of my father's wisdom, the way I went to Jim's house to have some fun. I knew my father could think of the right words. I tried to guess what they might be, maybe vocabulary words like *disenfranchised* or *misaligned*. Those words had to be good for something in such a fast-changing time.

But it was Denny who spoke next. "What about you, Jack? If steel goes, everything goes, is the way I see it." He paused. "Has to do with tension." Denny seemed to be turning a bit, turning toward an attitude that scared me.

"In steel," he kept on, almost sneering. "There's a point of *rupture*."

"Yes," my father said. "It's called the tensile strength."

"*It's called the tensile strength*," Denny said, deliberately. "Thank. You. Professor. The tensile strength."

Silence here. My blood went quicker. I eased my door all the way open.

"You got a union looking out for you up at that high school?" Denny continued.

"I would never trust a union," said my father, with exquisite care. Like an epitaph.

Something rattled the door. Maybe Denny was going to leave. But the rattle stopped, and his voice became louder, meaner.

"Professor says he wouldn't trust a union," said Denny. "Professor trusts his own sound mind and his pussy little job coaching the tennis team."

A beat of silence before my father spoke.

"Time for you to go."

"Time for me to go," Denny said. "Funny. You sound just like my boss."

"Denny." My father's voice was firm, no-nonsense. "You've been drinking. You've got some time to work this through. You don't have to decide anything tonight."

The phone rang suddenly. I didn't hear Denny or my father. I stepped into the hall, all the way in, and saw that Denny was turned towards the front door and was sort of twitching his hands, jumpy, and my father was between Denny and the door, with his hand on the doorknob. I saw my mother stepping towards Denny in the hall, in her quilted bathrobe. She started to speak.

But at that moment, Denny hauled back with his big asbestos fist and clipped my father on the jaw. My father hit the door with his head and his shoulders, and my mother made a sound like a puppy's yelp, and we both ran to the entryway and didn't know what to do. My father was slumped against the door, half-turned as though he would crawl through it, but he was not down on the floor. His glasses were crooked, hanging from one ear.

I looked at Denny and my arms shook. I wanted to pummel him with my fists, on the soft parts of his back and on his fleshy pink neck. The moment seemed to grow, but I said nothing. I was afraid my voice would sound loud and braying like an upset boy, and I wanted to be of more use than that. Misty Chantelle came into my mind, and I wondered what she would think I should do.

But what I did was also nothing, because my father's face stopped me somehow. He was on his feet again. My mother's hands were cupping his chin, and he spoke mildly.

"It's alright," he said. "Denny just forgot who he was."

He took off his glasses and wiped them with a handkerchief and put them in his pocket, where he usually kept his cigarettes. His jaw was red, and his mouth was bleeding a little, though he was speaking clearly. His hands were trembling, but not badly. He was a man intent on keeping his cool.

Denny looked at me and my parents and blinked his eyes. He stared at my father. The air seemed to go out of him and he looked like someone with no energy. He might have been dizzy, or sick, and I wondered too if my father felt all right. I didn't ask him, though. It felt like a moment between just the two of them. My mother stayed by my father, very close, but she was not holding him anymore. My father opened the door and stepped aside and Denny Cholovich went out into the cold.

—— /// ——

In the morning the silver Buick was not in the Cholovich's driveway. I walked to the bus stop with Jim as though it hadn't happened. Jim did not mention Denny or the closing of the mill. Later that day, I asked him if he knew that Denny had been to our house. Jim looked at me and shrugged his shoulders. He looked away and talked about something else. Springsteen, I think. We lasted the day.

Likewise, in my family, no one spoke that evening of Denny Cholovich or the night before, when he'd been to our house. As the days wore on, I would see him from time to time, in his driveway washing the car or hauling trash cans to the curbside. The robins returned, and each evening my mother filled the feeders in our back yard. We had a small locust tree just past the concrete steps that cast an arc of shadow on the grass beyond the patio light. One night as my mother stepped across that shadow to the feeder, I remembered a fragment she sometimes recited: *We made a circle that drew him in.*

And I realized that I had not seen Denny for a while. He and his Buick were gone. I asked Jim about it, and Jim said he had moved back to Duquesne, back with his mother.

"Really?" I said. "Why didn't you say something?"

Jim said, "Say what?" And then, "Denny who." I glanced over at him. He had a vacant, blank look, staring off in the direction of the river. I snapped my fingers and slapped fist to palm, and Jim let me race on ahead like an idiot.

We did not talk easily after that. He didn't have the time, he said, to go to the tracks or shoot pool. What had happened was beyond us, and we were not able to outreach it. Before long Jim and his mother moved away, and I got a short letter from him. They were with his aunt in Altoona. We wrote back and forth for a time and then they moved again and I lost track of the address. It was a year for mistakes.

My father coached the track season as always, but I remember he got old that spring. It was just life happening—there was a depletion about him that spoke of the teeth of things. He did not lose his job, like so many others did, at the mill and other places around our town. But I think he found little satisfaction in that. I remember driving with him through Homestead, on Saw Mill Run Boulevard, me behind the wheel, and we passed the twelve dormant smokestacks, the ones people called the twelve apostles.

Seeing them gave me a feeling of vacancy, loss. I thought of a steel cast gone awry, with white-hot metal shooting all over the place, a wasted and forlorn fireworks display. It was Denny who told me that blast furnaces were always named for a woman. The Dorothy, the Mary Ann. And how a century before, the Isabella beat Carnegie's Lucy furnace in a six-year production battle, waged at rival plants on opposite sides of the Allegheny River. The Isabella became the first furnace to pour a thousand tons of pig iron in a single week. "By the Thirties," Denny said, "we were pouring that much in a day." I can still see the quick flash of his gold chain. And how the story of the furnace battle seemed infused with a forward motion,

motion that could carry you far and make you a small part of something large and satisfying.

I wanted to tell the story to my father, but I didn't for fear he would ask me how I knew about it, and I would have to say Denny's name. Instead, I told him there was a girl at school who had been born by artificial incineration. He managed a smile. "I think," he replied, "you mean she was con*ceived* by artificial in*semi*nation."

My neck burned a bit at that—and at the thought that I could no longer be a kid who didn't know things and was happy not knowing them. I was grateful at least to have said something that was not about steel, not about the neighbors, not about the new, clean heaviness that hovered over the river towns. My father kept his eyes on the road. Before long we approached the turnpike. As I pulled out of the toll booth, he told me keep it on the double nickel.

And here's where the memory should shade off, into the gray morning, the leafless trees of this town's landscape. But it drives on, to where I had to take notice. That my father was a limited man. That he had somehow muscled Denny Cholovich's good sense away from him that evening, until Denny did not have the first clue whether to jump or sit tight. And sometimes you just hope that there's mercy. Trouble with unions and steel mills was trouble I would not begin to understand for years. It was so much larger than any of us were. But the weight of the words of one man to another can be equally large when one of those men is forced to a crossroads and can't tell where to turn. Though maybe, at great cost, toward a wiser man for help. I think of what my father said to Denny—words that seemed so benign and mild, words that were breezy and right but also were wrong.

A small thing? Perhaps. I remind myself, that mine is not to blame, that there are surely bigger mistakes you can make in a life. Just outside the window now is my honey-colored little boy, running across the backyard. His eager face turns to mine for direction, and approval. I watch as his sturdy legs clamber up that locust tree; I can still see the quick turns of his mind, the clear light in his eyes, how he is never yet with a thought that the day won't turn out to be a fine one. I don't know why my father said the things he did. I don't know that it was anything more than the regular bleakness that leaches into a heart. The hard energy, dry as feathers, that pushes forward at all expense.

Name

IN HIGH SCHOOL, I worked as a lottery ticket agent at a strip mall newsstand called Tri-State Book and Game. I was sixteen, seventeen, selling lottery tickets I was too young to buy or redeem, and I suppose such a situation is not so uncommon.

But it was a job that caused me some discomfort. Under the counter were the paper-wrapped *Playboys*, the *Hustlers* and *Blackguard* magazines. There were fragrant cigars in the boxes at my left hip. I didn't sell liquor—even beer was tightly controlled in Pennsylvania, you could buy it only from a distributor—but I peddled gambling, pornography, and nicotine like they were pure pulled taffy.

Again, not unusual, perhaps, except to say I was a Mormon girl growing up in the steel towns south of gritty Pittsburgh. On Mormon Day at Three Rivers Stadium, my parents hobnobbed in the loge with Pittsburgh native and former Allegheny County prosecutor Orrin Hatch, recently elected senator from Utah. Far below them, I sat steps away from the third baseline, a couple seats from Donny Osmond. I watched Hall-of-Famer Vernon Law throw the first pitch. My seminary teacher turned up and asked me, the stake president's daughter, to get an autograph from Donny, so I reached over and tapped the arm of his chair. I did not dare touch his wrist.

"Brother Osmond?" I handed him a program and a pen.

He asked my name, and I swallowed, shook my head. "It's not for me," I said.

Immediately, I worried I'd insulted him. When the truth was only that I was too shy to ask for an autograph of my own.

He nodded and signed the page. His hands were small, I noticed, as I took the program from him. Handed it back to my teacher.

Being Mormon meant I drove people home from kegger parties. It meant that when I accepted Christ as my personal savior at a born-again rally, I and the Campus Life youth leaders had to endure a firm reprimand from my father, who ushered us into his office in our living room. He told them in no uncertain terms that his daughter was not saved on a particular day, but every day, by the grace of Jesus Christ, after all she could do.

It meant I kissed David Toklas in his car in my driveway, home after a date to a PG movie. *E.T.* if I remember

correctly. Chaste, thin-lipped kissing. After an hour, David
went home.

———— /// ————

At the newsstand, a regular, a bit of a rough character—
moody, and changeable, whom I had privately given the
name Bruno—came in one day.

"Hello, doll," he said. He slipped a *Motor Trend* magazine off the rack and flipped through it. He called me doll
every day, and every day took his time browsing before
he played his numbers. Bruno made me uncomfortable:
whenever he arrived, the air got charged up with something new and electric. But it wasn't just that. It was also
his quick way of turning, with a grin or scowl, I never knew
which. Always sudden, a sort of shout.

A moment later, another man entered the store. A
large man, dressed in black leather and denim, his skin like
a polished buckeye. I became aware of the imbalance in
the room, like when you're on a bus and you realize you're
the only white person, or the one no longer young. It ticks
up your antenna a notch or two, though on that afternoon mine didn't extend to noticing this stranger as the
only black man in the shop. It did extend to the obvious
things—being small beside these two men, and timid in a
way I tried to conceal by standing very straight, making my
eyes bright, fooling nobody. Certainly to being just a girl;

and then I noticed his name. Stitched across the chest of his jacket in gold letters. Valentine.

Valentine's presence in the shop seemed to kick things into gear. Bruno quickly put down his magazine and snapped his fingers at me to get a number. Many of my customers got their picks from me, three digits for the Pennsylvania Daily Number. I knew they expected me to give them the first numbers that came into my mind. Thinking about the numbers—my birthday 5/23, my street address 149, the price of a *Hustler* $2.87—thinking the numbers made them contrived and freighted with use. I knew this somehow. My customers thought I was lucky, and though they weren't supposed to tip me when their numbers hit, they usually did. If any of them suspected I was messing with numbers in my head, even to give them a single thought, they would stop right there. They wouldn't buy from me, maybe not ever again. I'd be cold, beleaguered, no more white-tiger rare and lucky; they'd go down the street to Benny's.

But at the moment Bruno tried to extract my number, I looked away. Valentine's fingers rested on the edge of the glass countertop, and I noticed he was wearing a Super Bowl ring. I'd never seen one before, but I knew what it was. This was 1980, the heyday of the Pittsburgh Steelers, the closing year of the decade they won four of their six world championships. It would be decades before they'd win again. And I had one of the players, some kind of a blocker, I guessed from his size, or a linebacker; my brother would know who he was. I had Valentine, in the shop. A beat of time. Then I said the number from the ring: Fourteen, I said. Fourteen, and I threw in the number of the victory Super Bowls. Fourteen-four. One-four-four. Then I looked up.

Bruno paused a long moment. He cocked his head.

"Dolly, baby, you wouldn't mess with me now, hey? Just give me the number, straight out your head, doll, straight out your mouth here, see?"

I could feel a flush coming over my neck and shoulders. Being Mormon meant another thing: easily rattled. Wound a bit tight. One too many jokes about polygamy, or my mother's battered station wagon. Even now I can sometimes be made to feel I have wandered into a game of Shock the Mormon. Back then I was often embarrassed in my own skin, made vulnerable at the sound of my own name. *Lisbeth Thrush*. Spoken in anger by my mother, in blessing by my father. To be spoken, *Lisbeth*, in whispers by a sweetheart, on phone lines to receive news or congratulations. To be written on resumes and letters, contracts, in my checkbook. To think the sound of my name, to say it out loud could make me feel as fragile as a first-time lover. *Lisbeth*. My name.

Which Bruno pressed forward, across the countertop to remind or avail himself of. He leaned his head in toward me, my young-lady chest, bra size 32A—hoping for

C, I would settle for B—where I wore a plastic tag: *Lisbeth* in blue letters, a blocky footed script. I could see flakes of dandruff clinging to the roots of Bruno's hair. I could smell the product he put on it to keep it stiff and in place. I was frozen.

"*Lis Beth*," he said, very quietly, separating the syllables. There was a juiciness about the *s*. A puff of air after *th*, and I cringed with a shame I did not understand.

"What are we going to do with you?"

Valentine folded his newspaper.

I couldn't swallow. My throat was stuck. As if to acknowledge that, Bruno brought his hand up and pushed his finger on my mouth. His finger burned, it smelled like sausage. I dared not move, except to cut my eyes over at Valentine. Now there's a name. He stood formidable, hulking, not reading the sports page, his back turned to us. Could he be so tough with a name like Valentine? Or, I was hoping, how could he help but be.

He turned toward me then. Valentine. His deep voice rumbled out like an old hollow ache that's found its ease. He said, "I wonder you don't axe me fo' my auto-graph"—have I conjured this accent? but I don't think so, for it struck me as something to notice and remember.

I knew he'd watched me watching his ring. His eyes held me and I fumbled on the countertop for the stub of an old ticket—just a white slip of paper, the tickets were printed on a noisy machine; they had tractor-feed holes on the sides—and I slid it to him across the scratchy glass. He signed his name with a black marker, then pushed the paper back to me and asked for a ticket with the number I'd chosen: 144. I printed the ticket and handed it to him and put his dollar in my cash drawer. Slipped his autograph into the back pocket of my jeans, and then it occurred to me that might have been construed as a suggestive thing to do. Another helpless blush began to rise.

All of it felt like a lot of commotion, and somewhere in the midst of things Bruno had released me. Backed away from the countertop and resumed lurking near the magazines.

Valentine stayed a while longer, browsing. Finally Bruno went out the door and then Valentine did, and my knees managed to stop their clatter. The newsstand closed as the sun went down, and I locked the door with my silver key, my fingers still trembling, my mouth still bearing the singe of Bruno's finger.

——— /// ———

There was a girl at school named Candy Cotton. And a beautiful, self-assured girl by the name of Jason. A cheerleader, Wendy Peppersack. A boy everyone tormented: Donald Waczewski.

My interest in names could be traced to an older girl in our neighborhood, long since moved away. But not before I'd noticed her silver-blond hair, her long, racehorse legs.

And her name: Tonnie, short for Antoinette or Antonia, or so I thought, until I saw a newspaper article about her prowess in a local track event. It wasn't Antonia, not at all. Her name was spelled *T-a-w-n-y*. As in the color of our refrigerator. Or the suntan brushed in the cleavage of ladies in jacketed magazines at the newsstand. When I read Tawny's name, all the magic drained away. What power was this—what was it about names?

The Bible was full of people whose names the Lord changed. Abram to Abraham, Jacob to Israel. Sarai—Sarah. Saul, Paul.

There was a lady in our congregation—in our ward—who lived in Squirrel Hill. She had converted from Judaism, she married a Mormon Elder. They were expecting twins—hoping for boys—and her mother asked her what she would name them.

"We're thinking Peter and Paul," she said, "or maybe David and Daniel."

"Oh please," said her mother, "go with Peter and Paul. David and Daniel are much too Biblical!"

In my own house, no day felt complete until my mother heralded its close, with: "Shadrach, Meshach, and To Bed We Go."

The angel told Mary her child would be Jesus.

And there was my favorite. *Behold*, said the Lord, in the Book of Mormon verse I loved. *Behold, thou art Nephi, and I am God.*

Shawn Weatherly had lately become Miss America. Slim Pickens, Tiny Tim. Christmas Snow, Wilson Pickett, Molly Hatchet. Rosanna Rosannadanna, Mr. Bill, Jack Ham, Lily Rose, Linda Lovelace. Football great L.C. Greenwood, whom I always imagined as Elsie Greenwood. Holly Thornsberry, the name of a teacher I'd had in grade school, the most beautiful name I'd ever heard. Names spoken in whispers, with a caress; and again by the same people in a sneer, with rancor and judgment. Bruno spoke my name. And owned a piece of me he hadn't owned before.

——— /// ———

Outside the newsstand, I clutched the key in my fist, the sharp end lodged between my fingers. Protruding. This with the idea I could take a swipe at some attacker, at Bruno if need be. I made a show of walking briskly. I often wore a pair of heels with my jeans and I was beginning to feel the day's end, the tightness at my instep. Also a foolishness I could not quite put my finger on.

I focused instead on being quick, no-nonsense, and on the hard taps of my shoes on the asphalt, the slight echoing scritch of damp gravel beneath them. Rain had begun to fall. *Lis-beth*, my feet tapped. Right, left. Right, left.

The dusk deepened as I approached my car, a VW Bug I shared with my brother. A forlorn, hunched-over island on the glittering parking lot, one wheel straddling a painted line. The Bug had a two-toned paint job. One childish, rounded fender was forest green, while the rest of the car was tan and, I noticed in the streetlight, rusty. *Lis beth.* I kept hearing him. Lisbeth's car. It felt as though this was the only car in the lot, though that can't have been true. Other stores in the shopping center were open, and some had just emptied for the night like the newsstand.

I checked the far side of the car, peered in at the back seat, and all was clear. In a single motion, I twisted the key and opened the door. Got in and punched the lock down. The odor of cold vinyl and glass mixed with the oddly comforting smell of my brother's gym bag on the passenger seat. The windows began to fog.

This told me I was breathing, but my lungs felt heavy and flat. A terrible ache clenched at my shoulders, as though I'd been waked from a strenuous dream. But I knew I was physically safe, behind the locked doors of the car. I pushed my key into the ignition slot, and the certainty of the motion calmed me. I believed and was sure that I was fortunate enough, blessed, and lucky enough that he could not have lingered there.

Bruno.

Not his real name, which of course I never knew.

Still. Why not hurry and turn the key? Why not get the devil out of there and go home? Rain began to spatter harder, in fat drops on the windshield. Insistent and, as I sat, worsening.

In a moment I stopped thinking about Bruno. The weather had a heavy, calming effect, and soon I was not worried about him at all. I began thinking instead about my mother's name, and how my father would sometimes tease my mother, with the verses in the Bible written just for her.

"Shirley," he'd say, "the Lord God will do nothing, but he revealeth his secret unto his servants the prophets." Words so familiar they made a rhythmic harmony with the rain.

I smiled at the thought, so random and yet customary; I'd heard it at home twenty times. A small pleasure, to picture my parents and be relieved for a moment of the self-consciousness I could so rarely escape.

"Shirley. He hath borne our griefs and carried our sorrows."

Again, more than familiar, but somehow, after my close call, newly tender and funny and lovely all at once. A private family joke, with a sure foundation. Repeating the verse, I saw that with Valentine's help, I'd just negotiated a way through, or past, a potential sorrow. Surely.

At least part of the joke's effect had to do with what had been taught clearly in my home: that my father would one day call my mother's name in a way only she could recognize, through the sealing power. It would take place in another world, one far better than this. The idea had always unlocked a tender bloom inside me, just beneath my throat. And it did now, in the car while rain dropped in pellets on the roof.

But then another thought. Heavier, trickier. I swallowed carefully, as though within the sweetness of that bloom there was a scratchy splinter to be got past. The rain became a viscous, wide wash over the windshield.

It had to do with getting through the business with Bruno. There'd been rescue. Even a bit of preserved dignity. Here I was, safe in the car, protected—the same girl who'd left the car in the lot a few hours earlier. He had wanted something from me, perhaps, more than my name, and had not been allowed to take it.

But also he had done something to me. Or opened the knowledge of something having to do with me. I'd been slow to see it, but now I could not ignore it. Bruno, knowing my name. Using it to effect.

Me, not knowing his.

Back at the newsstand, those juicy magazines were never in view; still I sold a lot of them. Stacked upright under the counter, each of them was covered, cased in brown paper or with a kind of shellacked white cellophane. Their value diminished when the wrapper was slipped off by some anonymous man, the woman uncovered. And in some interior article or blurb, little as there was in the way of text, the woman named. To this day I'll notice a particular kind of woman, I'll *see* her on a bus, or while shopping: a slender, pretty woman walking into an office building, a loud, brassy woman herding children in a supermarket. I see them and I'm taken back—I'm young again—in my VW with the rain drumming all around.

But young as I am, I cannot discount the knowledge Bruno has awakened. I watch this woman as though I'm the girl in the car; and she is not to dwell or brood—she must not call attention to this smallish feminine suffering, its rules ridiculous and absolute. For a quick moment I have to resist asking her, so, when was it for you? At what point did you become aware? *Behold*, I imagine. Audacious, insisting. I take my woman's name—or hers, or any woman's name—place it in that Book of Mormon passage I loved so much, as though it could actually fit. *Behold, thou art Lisbeth . . .*

Finally I did drive out of there. The rain let up a bit, the way it does, and what could I do but keep my back straight, my knees pressed together. Click the ignition forward and make myself steer smoothly, carefully across the shimmering lanes. I turned up the heat, entered the flow of traffic. Focused on the pull, the shuttling, responsive thrum in the small engine when I shifted gears. I may have gotten lost awhile, taken some back roads. The sturdy Bug would have hugged the curves, its tinny purr working to cut the cool, wet fall of evening in a way that spoke to my agitation. Called up my resistance. At some point I would need to find a familiar highway home.

And in the solitary light of our foyer, I'd pause to slide the ticket stub out of my pocket. Valentine's autograph. Limp, and blurry from dampness. Then, walk into the glow of our family room, where everyone would be waiting for me. Drop it onto my brother's lap. As though he'd been the one with the right to it all along.

Jane's Journey

1. The Cottage Homes

TOM MUNDAY'S FATHER DIED YOUNG, but had given his son a name, and so a place in the cottage homes rather than the workhouse. Number Four, with seven other boys and six girls. The food was plain, just bread and dripping and coffee, but on Sundays a bit of potato, sometimes a steaming wedge of pork on a knife. And how Tom loved when winter came, to have the celery.

His master was a cobbler, and Tom came close to a career on a bench with the smart tools and implements. But he was small and quick and would dart noiseless under the table where there was a cat to play with, so the mistress owned he'd be better off in the fields, as he was close to the ground and short to bend. So Tom was caught up by a gangmaster and hired out near Countesthorpe, south of Leicester. Stone picking when the fields were put down for mowing, potato picking when the fields came up. "Get your back bent, Munday," the gang-man hollered. "There's no potatoes where you're standing." Tom got rid of a tendency to flinch, as he let the shouts roll over him. Early on he proved himself immune to beatings and insults, and in lesser ways indispensable, though he recalled the back pain all of his life.

By manhood, Tom was ruddy and had kept his quick, ducking laugh. He walked with a faintly perceptible bend, a gentle bowing of his round shoulders. He was not given to drink and he had the use of both strong arms and could bring in the barley with a single horse and three days. Any feral cat in the district could find him for a soft word and a share of his lunch.

He was what was thought of as "an every-day man"— common as a sunrise, but without which the world is made dark. And so he'd been taken on as tenant and caretaker for Louis Granger, who paid a fair wage, as high an advantage as a new draft horse for cutting soil.

There was a maid named Mariane also from the cottage homes, Number Two. Tom loved her the way all cottage-home boys loved: in a torment of silence and misery. She was shy and earnest, a sweet girl, well formed and of fragile build, and she sometimes drew a wanton gesture from a lesser man than Tom. This tortured him further, and he took to standing between her and the rougher rogue.

So Mariane trusted Tom; she helped him with his letters. She traded extra washing for lamp oil, a gift of time and labor he was never let to regard. She ironed by lamplight while Tom sat with her copybook and read her own careful sentences aloud to her, lines from other books she'd copied down, or verses written on her own. He never knew for sure which, and her vanity let him wonder.

And down the river's dim expanse,
Like some bold seer in a trance
Seeing all his own mischance
With a glassy—

She stopped him, with her quiet voice. "Mmmm love, that's *mis-chance*, not *mish-ance*." Tom looked hard at the verse.

"Thank you my dear," he said patiently. "But why mash the words together, and give a fellow a rum shot at the meaning?"

"Tis only the way of the writing," Mariane said. She pushed the nose of the iron into a corner seam. "It's not set about to confuse one, but to ask him to meet the word. Have an introduction if you like." She set down the iron and smiled at him.

"And next time you see it, you'll be old friends." She folded her smooth cloth and gave it a snap. Her eyes flashed warm, vivid, and relaxed. Tom turned back to the book.

And at the closing of the day,
She loosed the chain and down she lay . . .

One day just after third barley crop was laid in, he and Mariane stood side-by-side. He was sunburned and scrubbed, she held a clutch of wild carrot and choke-flowers. Laughing with relief and gladness and fear, they recited vows before the vicar, who presented the gift of an ivory damask tablecloth, though they had no table.

Before a year had gone, Walter was born to them, and Tom had a place as a tenant farmer. As the years slid by, he nursed in himself the pride of a landowner, though truly he owned just the chance to husband Granger's fields and fill Granger's dray with milk cans heavy with Granger's milk. In their tiny cottage on Granger's farm, Tom hoped for more sons to make his work light and expand his reach. And he dared even to imagine a daughter with the same ginger hair as her mother, the same creamy skin and consoling voice. While they rarely spoke of this, he would sometimes come upon a sadness in Mariane's shoulders as she set about some task. He watched the slim curve of her bodice as she reached for eggs in the straw.

"Tomorrow, maybe," he would say in his mind, and he dropped a kiss on the back of her neck. "There remains time yet my sweet one." And finally on a bitter, rain-soaked autumn eve, branches scratched at the window glass and Tom bent over Mariane in the dark. He broke his silence, began to whisper how there was time still, and she smiled, shushing his mouth with her finger.

"Time indeed," she whispered. "I am almost afraid to tell! But Tom, see." He could just make out the tiny sparkle in each of her dark eyes. Her feeling had outrun her modesty, and she placed his hand low on her belly. "I fancy a new little one, started and growing there, even now."

He felt nothing but the soft and typical, lovely oblivion of her skin in the dark, then the knob of a hip bone as she turned toward him. He laughed against her neck, against the flutter of her voice, and said she would soon be as stout as a cucumber. He was only a little surprised when she proved right about her claim, and on a bright morning that next March delivered a little girl.

Quickly, then, those sunrises stacked themselves into years of energy and tranquility. The boy grew taller, and the baby girl seemed to want to catch up. Farmhand and wife. Son, then a daughter. For working alongside, Tom preferred his son above all others, and he doted on his daughter; and Mariane on all of them, and on her flowers and grapes and her goats and the soft cheese they made, which she was permitted to sell every Thursday at market, and keep the proceeds for the family.

In the evenings, spent with work and dull-witted with hunger, Tom walked toward the rough house Granger had built on the far west corner of his farm. The cottage was close and dimly lit, small and damp. A single thin wall separated them from the chicken shed, which he himself had built, with walnut planks and plaster. But a glow lifted off it in the evening light. Inside waited Mariane, their son Walter, and Jane, this narrow-faced, trim little daughter. Ordinary. But the ordinary was more than Tom had seen for his own future or thought to hope for, and he felt he had stumbled into a luck more than pretty and not of his making. He whispered, *old Tom of the cottage homes, ye are a family man, and it is well ye've done for yourself here.*

2. Letters

My dearst Walter, Simon Roorsall is returned to us. Though he joined The Battles three months before you called up to fight, his enemy was not the forces of the Russian Czar but the typhus, got in by way of a leg wound. He has only a pant leg now, folded beneath the thigh. He is lifted each morning to the tall seat of Granger's carriage and does never get down but waits reins in hand while Granger attends his business. Roorsall was here last Saturday to fetch your mother back to Mrs. Granger's. Thin as a stalk of wheat, with the same pale color, and I asked how did he fair. Called up to battle, Guvnor, he said, and sure a bloke like I would be in bits due to the cannon fire, and my name in the paper. So this is nothing but a bonus. A man can do without his leg. I made no reply but nodded my head to agree. Keep your noggin ever clear. Remember your prayers. Yours, Father.

To Tom Munday by urgent post. Mrs. Munday is wanted for the spinning. A carriage will call Friday before noon. Yours in trust, Louis Granger.

To Tom Munday by urgent post. Mrs. Munday is wanted for the raspberries, for jelly and syrup. Yrs in trust, Louis Granger.

Dearst Walter of the Battles. Your mother owns Granger's wife has become a broken winged sparrow who can never leave its nest. Though she has use of both her legs. If we can believe Granger, Roorsall got the typhus sure at the cooking camps, where food was assembled for the fighting men. So here is a joke that is not a joke. You must stay out of the camps, they are full of disease and disrepute, and keep forward in The Battles where it is safest. Put your head always straight and watch for scullybuggers, you have learned to get the best of them. Remember your prayers. Father.

Tom folded this note into a sleeve and pressed it with a great black stamp heated in the fire, which he pounded with a single solid *thump.* Then turned the paper to touch his lips to Walter's address. *River Danube. The Battles.*

Dear Mr. Tom Munday, please make Mrs. Munday available as she is wanted at the house. L Granger.

Jane's mother had been gone, she had *been wanted* now, five days' time.

My dearst Walter. I am sure you would like to here news of the village, but it will have to wait. Mrs. Granger is taken with the ague and sent for your mother. Jane is a smart cook in her absence and can boil a chicken with parched corn and potatoes or beans with salty bacon. The cobbler was black on the lower crust as you prefer, and Jane owned she thought of you while it cooked. The butter is sweet but scarce as Mother sells all she can at the green, add to that Coral never gives the milk as she did for you. Fever and pox in the camps is the talk of the papers. Rest as sure on the account of the smallpox. Granger tells the mercy as though he ordained it himself, since you have had the cow pox from Coral, you cannot get the smallpox. Remember to pray, I ever shall. Your Father.

To Tom Munday. Urgent. Mrs. Munday is wanted. A carriage to call this evening. In trust, L. Granger.

Dearst Walter of the Battles If you could see your sister you would laugh to the belly ache, she kept back carrots from the soup and we hold them like cigars you see at the most hearty pubs and talk at one another. There, see, I tell her, you will marry a poor farmhand with no land of his own and no manners in the bargain. She waggles the green feathertop outside her lips and slips her eye toward heaven, aye, she'll say, nor shall his mistress carry any. I'm glad since we have been at pains to make Jane smile, it is too long since we here from you. Pls send report without delay and always remember your prayers. Your Father.

To Tom Munday. Mrs. Munday is wanted. A carriage will call. Yrs in constancy. Granger.

Jane watched as her father read the note and stared long at the fire. Her mother, pale and silent of late, was in the barn milking Coral. Tom licked his finger and pinched a matchstick of wood from the edge of the fire. He brought it slowly toward the note and let the flame touch Granger's white scrap and furl it slowly in on itself until it was a thin petal of black ember. This he dropped onto the brick hearth, and a wisp of smoke trailed up in the cool of the room, like a consolation. Jane stirred the cornmeal harder and put extra butter in the tin.

3. Granger

She spoke softly to his wife Therese, and he took to finding reasons to come into the house so he could hear the placid rise and fall of Mariane's voice. When she made tea for Therese Granger, she brought him a cup as well. There was a certain look given at the end of the exchange of the cup, a glance when her eyelids dropped. A rise of shoulders, a turning and preening about her neck, which she sometimes touched with her fingers. It was the motion he fancied he knew well: that of a woman conscious of being watched.

He knew this about women. They either provide these looks and glances or they have found the way to shut them off, the way you shut off ditch water with a canvas dam. It is nothing to do with manners or conversation or smiles, which can be in plain sight, and the canvas dam patched firmly into place. He turns away from such a woman, every time. Granger is a man used to single-minded work, to the business of running his farm, his careful notions of crops and seed and dairy prices and the shipping of goods to Birmingham by coach or train.

But a *glance* could make him feel that those strivings had been noted and found exceptional. That he had been measured, that his measure was quality. And if that glance were seasoned with a kind of tremulous tension, well. It was another kind of measure altogether.

When Mariane Munday was sent for, his house improved almost immediately. Though he always employed a cook, now the pots and pans were relieved of a sheen of grease. The curtains and bed linens were aired, and a broom found its way under beds and into shadowy corners. She poured a cupful of cool water into soil, and the flowers seemed to instantly lift their heads. He took to calling for her often.

She was a proper housemaid indeed. Yet something about her not quite spotless. Something of the ribald dairymaid there, for all her calm manners, her clean habits, her quiet speech. She was after all a girl from the cottage homes. Mariane Munday. Her name fitted together like a bolt and a nut, like a sugar jar and its lid.

No village voice was ever raised in Mariane's censure or defence. Nobody ever warned her, no one accused her, nobody came to her rescue, no citizen called her to account. She had that pretty cottage with its flowers, and she kept her looks, and she held tight to a reserve, a privacy that looked to them like aloof, though it wasn't the same. Tom was an amiable man, too decent a man, common enough for a cuckold. "Where's the missus, Munday? Up to the big house again?"

As for Mariane herself, what was she to do? A home. Steady work. Children in school. *We have the work so they can rise,* she told Tom often enough. All of this dependent on a landowner as much as on a good, strong workingman for a husband. Granger was a man she knew she should despise, and she did despise him. But that didn't entirely cancel out something of gratitude for him, something of obligation. Obviously there was something about her that invited reproach.

Could you ever imagine you might need a man who was not your husband so desperately? Did you ever suppose you could come to love two men at the same time? Look well, my dear. You can.

4. A Door

Jane was almost fifteen, and wearing a linen dress she would never tire of, dyed the same blue as the bachelor buttons that grew where the barn met the earth. Her father Tom was walking toward the barn to put up the horse, Shylock. Her mother was home, a day or even two earlier than Tom had expected. The soft light of dusk cleaved from the yard.

Wheels drove in slowly from the field road. Tom looked up to see Mr. Granger sitting atop a wagon instead of a buggy, the wagon pulled by two magnificent oxen. Granger was a tall man with a trim beard and a farmer's marketing suit. No matter the weather, Granger cut a fashionable figure. Today, on the back of his wagon, he had loaded a door.

"A fine evening, sir, no rooks in the corn," Tom said by way of salute.

"Ye've checked every row, I'd wager?" replied Granger, with a laugh. "Lord bless em to fly off forever, and without my harvest in the bargain."

"My Jane here. She runs through the rows and gives them a frightful presence," said Tom. "Look at her, will you. She's a fearsome sight."

Jane stood in the eave of the barn door. Her summer lessons—taught by her mother—were finished; the eggs had been gathered, the patch of string beans weeded and raked. In the crook of her arm she held a rabbit.

Granger sat with his hands on his knees. "What a pretty picture you make, my girl, next to those blue flowers." He paused, and said to himself, "Fearsome perhaps, yes. But not to the crows." Jane clutched the rabbit so tightly it jumped and ran into the grass.

Tom's chest clogged with discomfort as Shylock tossed his smart head. It was one thing for Mariane to be gone for days at a time, an ordeal Tom scarcely allowed himself to recognize. Now he had admitted, even encouraged the man to address his daughter. He tightened Shylock's harness and a buckle jangled.

"Perhaps Mrs. Munday would appreciate a new door on the cottage." Granger swept an arm back to indicate the load on the wagon bed. "Or a bedframe made from a door, for her fair daughter. At all rates, it's yours to do as you like."

In the wagon bed, a flat, well-made piece of lumber rode. Tom put a hand to the back of his neck. Studying the ground, said he supposed it to do him more good than toast and ale, but was loath to be obliged.

Granger insisted. His did not make a present of the door, but a payment. "You are to think on it as a bonus," he said. "The twin goats that were saved in the spring." This had been a difficult birth, enabled by Tom. "The milk they'll provide, for Mrs. Granger. Call it a portion of harvest." And Granger winked at Jane, who stood hugging the barn as if were a great, sheltering person.

Tom allowed that he'd prefer to keep the cottage as it was. There was hardly need for a door, they'd be pressed to the walls. But Granger had climbed down and now turned to the back of the wagon, and Jane saw that her father had somehow been deflected. She watched as Tom lifted one end of the door off Granger's wagon and centered it over a small wooden dolly with stone wheels. He pushed the dolly under the wagon and signaled to Granger, who gave a single *hyuh* to his oxen and brushed a whip across the ridge of their backs. They blew a complaint, but nodded and lumbered forward, and Tom eased the door to a center moment on the dolly. Granger lifted a hand and turned the wagon round the yard. On his way.

They had a few days before Granger's barley cleared. In a spare hour each night, Jane stood with her father in weak slants of light as it entered the barn. She pressed her body against the wooden door to hold it steady against a post, while he shaved and planed the long lines of walnut.

"A peace-able grain," Tom called it. He meant that the wood could be planed from either direction. Curls of wood frothed at the blade of the adze, and sawdust motes danced in the light. She took a rasp to bevel the edge of a rough corner, as he had taught her, while he worked at a rough circle cut from a piece of smooth applewood. This was to fit where a doorknob might have gone.

Jane could see that the door would make a pretty table, one to be finished in time for the haysel supper. Then, Mr. Granger would make them a present of a turkey and some bacon. The barn smelled of hay and rain and animals and unwashed work. It held the cluck and flutter of roosting chickens. Her father, whistling, wielded his own thin rasp like a wand of silver as he trimmed the circle in the shaft of light. Stacked carefully in a corner were the dove and tail ends of joints cut from applewood for the table's base.

The heating of brandy for the finish was a delicate task, one Jane would remember all her life. "You'll never have a fire near a barn, my pretty maid." Tom had said it thirty times if he'd said it once, so Jane carried the brandy in a small tin creamer from the cooking fire in their cottage. She crossed the blade of light from near the barn's high window, the light like a window itself as it caught the wood of the new table.

"My maid has spilt nary a drop, I'm sure," he said, as she drew closer. Jane had covered the cup with a cloth and held it tight, but still a bit of the liquid had splashed her hand and her boots.

"Hardly spilt, Father," she said. "But not nary."

He caught her eye and winked. She poured the cup of warmed alcohol into a bowl of liniment oil and pine resin—all borrowed from Mr. Granger's stores. Took up a peeled twig and stirred. Steps away, Tom worked the wood until the cut circle fit the door like a snug cork in a bottle. Where the circle had been sanded—Jane's task—the applewood took on a burled glow, a pale, fisted knot for a plate or a mug to rest.

"That's my beauty," Tom told her, pointing to the circle. "A grand job for a little miss."

She dipped a cloth into the mixture and touched it to the planks, where it turned the wood a brighter, deeper shade. They worked quietly, Jane rubbing the finishing liquid in narrow bands along the smooth planes. The table's surface was shot through with a flourish of purple black, like the flash of a bay pony.

"It can't resemble a door any longer, Father," she said, finally. Her words came seldom but easily with him, where with others they were apt to lodge in the space between her throat and her lips. Tom Munday gave her a fond look and whistled The Fox Amidst the Hens.

Then came the night they first set the table in the cottage. What had seemed snug was crowded now, and they pressed their chairs against the wall that looked on the fireplace. Mariane set a pot of goldenrod on the table's center. She poured fresh coffee and set out early apples, warmed and sliced, piled in tin saucers of cream, and sat with the two of them at table, knitting a muffler for Walter at the front. Light from the fire grew dim, and shadows flickered tall and soft-edged. The air grew colder, thinner. Tom said "I guess we'll spare another log before this evening's up." He placed it and sat back. It was long before any of them moved to go to bed.

5. Such As Your Life

Rain fell, deepening every fragrance and softening speech. Bachelor buttons shone bright against the green and the mud. Simon Roorsall reached beyond Jane's waist to snap off a six-inch stem and presented it with a flourish. "Did you use these to color your eyes?"

He was more nimble than she could have imagined, having got down from the driver's box somehow, despite his missing leg. Now he's catching water from the barn's eaves for his horses; a moment later he stands with his elbow in the crook of a peeled sycamore staff. Supported in this way, he could hold the water to the horses, in the same leather bag he used to feed them oats or corn.

She kept her eyes on his face rather than his leg. It was brown and smooth, wet with raindrops. As he smiled, his dark eyes went curved and flashing, like fishing lures.

"Does it hurt, where your leg was?"

"Itches like a hornet. I go to scratch it, and then I remember."

"Will it grow back?" she said, and then looked away.

"Oh, aye," he said, "it will, sure. When pigs rise up out of the barnyard." She met his voice with an apology in her eyes. "About the time you lose your pretty looks," he continued. "Which is to say, never." He gave her a quick grin to show he was not insulted.

"I did not mean to be foolish," she said. "I only meant to say, you are young to have such a loss. I only meant to say it's good that you lost nothing more. Such as your life."

Roorsall had unhitched his horse from its carriage. He slapped his rump. The horse had learned to take his orders without being led and trotted easily into the Munday barn.

"If I had lost my life," he said. "I'd not care much, as what would I know about it. But since I have my life, I never think in the least of my leg."

"There's a riddle for me," said Jane. "You mean you are glad you lived."

She was close to tears. Her father Tom had not lived, and no word from Walter for weeks. Tom had been felled by Shylock the beloved horse, who moved forward when he should have halted, or halted when he should have moved forward. Quick as silver, a Jackson pitchfork took Tom's back for a load of sweet barley hay. Tom, no longer fully in this world, lay in his bed for two days; and then, fully gone to the next, was laid out for the third day on the table he and his daughter had made.

Yet here was a man speaking softly to her, a man who knew as well as she how thin the dividing curtain was. One side held your pains and aches, disrupted sleep, sorrow. Such as your life, such as no longer your life.

Roorsall spoke again. "So many men fared worse, it's no good to give this old stump another consideration. Gladness enters into it not at all. Glad has naught to do with living or dying. When I see you by this barn, though, as when we learned my letters by the fire, it's then that gladness enters the picture."

6. Mormons

Tom talked of them before he died; they were the talk of the village by the time Jane and Simon Roorsall wed. Two men in threadbare clothing, with a small leather book claimed as come from an angel. Two men maligned in every which way, as was any bugger with the misfortune to be accosted by them.

You heard tell. They are of Christ, they are nothing of Christ. They pretend the words of our Lord, never in the way of our Lord. A bell chimed, calling the penitent to chapel. Oh *God*, said one. You hear that? *That's* of Christ.

If that's of Christ I've heard it all my life, and what a nuisance!

Or has it been for the better?

Aye, for the better, you lout, you think you couldn't have sunk lower than you are?

So how then do they say *their* words are of Christ?

Go and hear for yourself.

Christ! I'm not coming near them. Jesus Joseph and Mary, not going near them for love or life! Not as your soul's your own . . . you read their book, and then they've got you. ·

But then it was told that a good woman on the north side of Countesthorpe became a believer, and after that her devil of a husband and four of her children. Baptisms were kept quiet, but Jane managed to learn they were held in the cool silk of Bailey Pond, past Mittersand's blacksmith shop; she dreamed of the water closing over her head and washing her clean. She was not sure what dirt was found in her soul, but she knew she thought poorly of her mother sometimes, and at other times she laid off her work and dreamed, causing more work for another. She knew further that she wanted to rise, to put her learning to use, to become more than a tenant farmer's daughter or wife; and she couldn't think how this might be accomplished.

Soon came talk of gathering Saints—Mormons—in western America. The journey of a lifetime, and no coming back. Mormons across the ocean would lend the money for the journey, and be paid with toil and sweat in the valley of the Salt Lake, which nobody wanted, and so the Mormons could have.

And why would they take such a valley?

Before his death, Tom answered that one. "For a kingdom they're building, one that lasts beyond this world. Aye, and I'd go were I a younger man," he'd said. "Take my family and build a better world. Perhaps we'll go, my Jane. Think of it!"

Jane could see him in her mind's eye, as though he sat in the tiny parlor with her. He knocked his fist on his bent knee and spoke.

"That slattern Farnsworth," Tom had said. "Washed clean in our Lord, trying a new start. How long will that take, I wonder. Yet the words they use is live up to your privileges. Live up to yourselves, your privileges. Farnsworth! Nothing beyond a clout on the head for all his days." He stopped to stir the fire with an iron poker. "Think of it!" She could hear his savage whisper rise. In spirit, or memory, some fresh combination of the two, Tom was almost, almost in the room. "Think, my girl. Where the Mormons are, you own your soul yourself."

—— /// ——

Farnsworth, lover of grog and newly born of water in Bailey Pond, held for himself a beer party. The party was spread about his rattletrap front porch and sod, the night before he and his Sally were to depart. Many of the village men were there.

Loud and insufferable with drink, John Farnsworth was. Sally stepped out the front doorway, her clothing packed. A washboard was tied to her sack at a crazy angle, a baby latched onto her hip and another pulled at her skirt. Evidently she had invited herself to the beer party.

"Be ye sailing wi' us to America, Johnny Farnsworth? Or be ye staying here?"

"Why chance it Johnny?" said a bilious man with a leather pouch slung across his shoulder. "Ye've friends here, and work."

"And aught to drink!" came another voice.

"The sea swallows those wi' red hair, Johnny," he heard. "Stay here and let your missus go."

"What about my children," said Johnny, who began his question in a laugh, as though glad to be rid of them, but finished it choked in a high and strangled voice. "They got my flaming hair, more's the pity!"

"Curse on a sailing ship, we all heard tell," they cried. "Stay here, Johnny Farnsworth. Stay wi' us!"

"I'm going, Johnny," said Sally, and she marched toward the wagon. "Sure, I've sewed our tickets in my shirtwaist. God be with me, and God with you, be you here nor there. I'm going wi' the Mormons, and God won't sink our ship. The captain says if there's Mormons on board, he always gets through."

The first firefly took Johnny's glance. He palmed the fine strawberry hair of his tallest girl. She smiled at his low voice. "I'll be going wi' ye, my Sal. I'm off wi' ye to America."

The men in the yard sent up a warbling shout. Soon big blinkered horses with feathered hooves pulled them past fields, the ditch, past the stable with Arclay's boot-black, down the dark roads.

The first miracle of our Lord had turned water into wine, Jane knew. A conversion of the very elements of matter, as thrilling as if Farnsworth's mug of beer had become tea with milk and the sweetness of honey. Yet that miracle was nothing, really, when compared to a message that turned men's action. A message from our Lord himself, who'd been silent with grief, with consternation, for hundreds of years. Up the country, in a lighted square in the town, at a pub near the coach line came the whisper. The Mormons were gathering.

7. Can You Drive a Team?

There is a Leicestershire record of Jane's brother, Walter Munday, gone to war in the Crimea. If Walter survived and returned to the tenant farm near Countesthorpe, he found his family dead or scattered. The ship's bill at Harper's Ferry, Missouri lists only this: *Jane Munday Roorsall, widow.*

When she reached Harper's Ferry, just west of St. Louis, July 1856, Jane was without family, friends, or money. She'd used the money to bury her family as they traveled from New Orleans, dead one after another from cholera. Mariane Munday first, then Simon Roorsall, and finally her baby Adelaide Thomasina Roorsall. Each listed on the customs manifest of Orleans Parish, and not one of their names written on the Missouri shipping bill.

The Mormons in the camp were wary. They had been burned out, starved out, driven out of Kirtland, Ohio; and then Jackson, Missouri; Nauvoo, Illinois; and Kanesville, Iowa. Worn from grief and milk fever, Jane approached wagonmaster Milo Andrus at Harper's Ferry. She asked to join his company as it traveled west. Andrus was leaving in thirty-six hours.

"Can you drive a team?" he asked her.

She faced Milo Andrus, at age 18 and four months, having lost a brother, left a home, borne and buried a baby. She'd survived a crossing, cared for a failing mother, nursed a dying husband, grieved the loss of five loved companions. A photograph taken in later years reveals a slight woman: dark hair and light eyes and a downturned mouth.

Could she drive a team.

Whatever her tone as she answered, it did not dissuade Milo Andrus. It persuaded him to give her a place in the company, and later, to make her his seventh wife. Seventh wife is a certain and shocking fact, and a story for another day. As far as facts go, I don't know if Granger threatened the family, or how Tom died. If Roorsall believed in God or the hope of a spiritual kingdom, gathering in America. I don't know if Jane's brother Walter ever tried to find them, or if her eyes were blue, or if Mariane taught Tom to read.

I don't yet know how Simon Roorsall died.

I've had to build these scenes from scanty narratives long on piety, short on details. This story is short on piety, but perhaps that is only true at first glance. The physician Luke put it this way: *Lo, we have left all, and followed thee.* Another story might give Jane all the credit. Or blame, depending on how you saw it. Jane—*Jane*—who launched and carried that faith, across ocean and rivers and over Great Plains on a wagon train, to be handed down like an album leaf, faded but substantial.

But perhaps Jane is not the story. The story belongs to Mariane and Tom, at the fireside with their daughter in their tiny tenant cottage, pressed nearly to the walls by Granger's table. Goldenrod drops pollen onto gleaming, finished walnut. A soft rain falls outside. Tom has finished his letter to Walter, and Mariane knits a muffler. Tom is a man who spreads light and cheer all around him. Mariane has acquired a certain gravity. She has become aware of men not so decent, men who draw her to them in spite of herself, and this gnaws at her soul. Shadows flicker on walls, across their faces.

What options are theirs, as hooves and carriage wheels roll into the yard? Granger has his eye already on their daughter. The situation is desperate, but not more desperate than the moments of almost any life. When Tom is taken, what could Mariane and her daughter do but take the chance, the hope that was offered and proved so durable, spun like gold through generations of time and trouble. When charged, or blessed, with such a hope, what can anyone do? What can I do, but grab hold.

Lucin Trestle

Southern Pacific Ltd, Great Salt Lake
New Year's Eve Sunday, 1944

THE WAR was all but over, everybody said. Who failed to inform Luxembourg? The Germans drove hard and the 109th held fast, only to lose four of every five men who wore the Keystone patch. Bloody bucket men. Charley Mougham checked out at Clerf castle in the fire, went down shooting. Lieutenant Welland had either seen it or been told, he couldn't say for sure.

Sixty thousand green-troop reinforcements—"salt waters," by decree no longer called replacements—arrived in the Ardennes within a week. Snow was drifting at eight feet, but the freezing boxcars got through, with blankets as well as men. They carried boots, canned peaches and tins of ham, reminders of a regular world. It was decided that salt waters would not be integrated with the more seasoned soldiers: "too destructive for morale." Instead, the remains of the 109th and the 110th, which had fared even worse, got sent home. Damn lucky to make it out. Everybody said.

On that long retreat, Lieutenant Welland followed the news as carefully as you could from limping convoys, from telegraphed, chalked notices on a ship that listed constantly to the port side. He'd lost twenty ill-afforded pounds and full use of his left hand, which he kept gloved and curled around a rubber ball. It was in Belgium that he lost the ability to sleep for more than an hour, two at the most. By Liverpool, he dreamed with his eyes open: falling from a whistling plane into rock-riven ice fields, snowmelt running pink with blood. Across the Atlantic, he dreamed of the whitewashed, crumbling castle, filling slowly with rock dust and fire. Through the coal-black landscape of Pennsylvania—Charley's home—and over Indiana, then past Chicago, he spun out of daydreams in a sweat, a fever, couldn't think where the train was. He'd lost the memory of prayer. Lost the taste for food and forced himself to swallow the sandwich a civilian pressed on him just outside Laramie. He downed a warm glass of tomato juice and clenched his jaw to keep from retching.

What had he gained? A fear of time. An antipathy to leisure or wastefulness, to waiting—he could do it in a tent, in a foxhole, behind a block of gray snowbank; it had become impossible on a train. He was jumpy, wary, overalert; it seemed to him he had no patience at all. So used to not zipping his fly he caught himself seated in a full passenger car with it gaping open. In his bag were a well-stropped razor, a nickel-sized cake of soap he'd hoarded and wrapped in burlap, and a tiny, round brush of horsehair, which he could still clutch, if he fit it just so, in the claw of his damaged hand. There were patches of snow in his beard, which he planned to shave carefully away at the last stop before home, if his nerves could manage the task.

―――― /// ――――

ON THE FINAL STRETCH he boarded a Pacific Limited, eighteen cars, and left Ogden, Utah well before dawn in a charcoal fog. The train heaved forward and lumbered west across Great Salt Lake. Out the dark window were the barest outlines, crusty banks of snow and mud alongside the trestle like dead sheep, and beyond those banks the slow jostle, the gelatin slush of water. The view was the same on either side of the train. All was muted, frozen; he blew on his fingers and rubbed a clear spot on the window. It steamed over, obscuring and then revealing a haggard face he failed to recognize. Seventeen miles tucked beneath his feet in twice as many minutes.

It was Sunday; someone on the train mentioned this, and in an instant, the kitchen in Granite Cove was warm and close. Woodsmoke and salt pork; his mother tilting a mound of onions onto a flat griddle. For the first time, he took note: she'd always stayed home from church to prepare dinner for the family. Before the war, the Sabbath had been a day apart, for starchy clothing, taking stock. No ceremony on this Sunday morning, but Lt. Welland found that fragments of old hymns still entered his mind. *As thy days may demand. Ye simple souls who stray.*

Down went the gunner, the bullet was his fate. Down went the bombardier, and now the gunner's mate. He squeezed the hard rubber ball. *Step forward soldier.*

He felt a bump, and then the train lurched. It seemed to take an awful plunge right, and then a sharp cast upward, and Lt. Welland heard the low, awful groan of metal on metal. There was time to hear the groan turn into a snarl, and the train became noise. Lt. Welland was buried in sound. He gasped, and clamor filled his lungs; he had time to wonder rather than flinch at the bitter, hot pain, hardly time to resist but only somehow to regard.

A thought came to him: *to survive twenty months in an artillery battalion,* but very quickly it didn't matter. There was the taste of metal as it slammed and subsumed Lt. Welland's face and skull. His smooth-shaved jaw and neck folded neatly into chrome and cloth and steel. Shoulders, blue cloth, felt hat, close-cropped hair, brain and ears, the cords at the back of his neck, the clackety bones of his spine, his ropy forearms, his pure, clean, perfect lungs, his churning heart and tiny and intricate trailways of blood, the crimson sinews and shining, youthful organs now tangled and blended, melded, heated, transmogrified into iron and fog and cloth and time and passengers.

He came to himself beside the train, standing somehow on the churned up ice and froth of the lake. The great clatter was cut off from his hearing, as though he'd been plunged into water, and the fog became lighter, arid, soft. He felt rather than saw that his limbs were free: not mangled and bound in steel, but buoyant, tinged with energy. He was warm.

He could just make out the Pacific Limited locomotive, two cars forward, plowed into a slowed caboose on the line ahead in the fog. The train he'd boarded less than an hour ago, now before and beside him, twisted and thrust beneath the first train's caboose and almost a full railcar. He watched as the trains wrestled one another, tugged and careened, then came to rest on the mud flat causeway lapped on either side by Salt Lake. How beautiful and terrible the crumpled train and the strangers still on it, living and dying in moments and spheres he'd outreached. His foxhole buddy, Charley Mougham—*step forward, soldier*, how many times he'd heard Mougham say it, and now—Mougham was somehow nearby. There was no mistaking the scent of damp wool and cinnamon chewing gum. Lt. Welland's mother seemed close, his silent, severe coal-miner father as well. All with him and standing in the thick, oily lake; and yet, too, were his parents safely ahead in the little stucco house outside Granite Cove, now likely planning their drive to the station to pick him up.

A hand gently took his supple left hand—tender, silvery touch—and he knew these were the slender fingers of Constance, his baby sister, died of a fever when he was six; he understood she'd been with him at Clerf castle. He turned to the sound of her voice and found that she stood at the point of a beckoning time and place. Her surroundings seemed to him of greatest consequence, a realm, a state of understanding, in the same moment warm and cool, robust and tender, vast yet intensely personal, weighty and buoyant, generous but also exacting, shot through with fire and reckoning—yet drenched in a watery, green glade of patience.

Step forward, soldier.

HEIDI NAYLOR'S essays and stories have appeared in the *Washington Post*, the *Idaho Review*, *Portland*, the *Jewish Journal*, *Sunstone*, *Dialogue: A Journal of Mormon Thought*, and other venues. She teaches English at Boise State University.

www.ingramcontent.com/pod-product-compliance
Lightning Source LLC
Chambersburg PA
CBHW061232170626
46809CB00007B/2634